THE HIDDEN WORLD OF
Changers

No. 3: The Power Within

by H. K. Varian

Simon Spotlight

New York London Toronto Sydney New Delhi

SIMON SPOTLIGHT
An imprint of Simon & Schuster Children's Publishing Division
1230 Avenue of the Americas, New York, New York 10020
This Simon Spotlight edition September 2016
Copyright © 2016 by Simon & Schuster, Inc.
Text by Ellie O'Ryan
Illustrations by Tony Foti
All rights reserved, including the right of reproduction in whole or in part in any form.
SIMON SPOTLIGHT and colophon are registered trademarks of Simon & Schuster, Inc.
For information about special discounts for bulk purchases, please contact Simon & Schuster
Special Sales at 1-866-506-1949 or business@simonandschuster.com.
Designed by Nick Sciacca
The text of this book was set in Celestia Antiqua.
Manufactured in the United States of America 0816 FFG
10 9 8 7 6 5 4 3 2 1
ISBN 978-1-4814-6964-7 (hc)
ISBN 978-1-4814-6963-0 (pbk)
ISBN 978-1-4814-6965-4 (eBook)
Library of Congress Catalog Card Number 2015954651

Impundulu

Hailing from the southern tip of Africa, the impundulu is a massive bird of prey that can control the weather at will, summoning fearsome storms.

Its immense wingspan and connection to the weather has made this Changer a master of the skies. With a flap of its wings, the impundulu can cause a powerful gust of wind or an earth-shattering clap of thunder. Lightning bolts can be channeled through the body and redirected with its talons.

Though the ability is rare, powerful impundulus can generate electricity within themselves. This energy can be used in the Changer's human form to create force fields and fire off lightning bolts whenever needed. For this reason, the impundulu is perhaps the most powerful fighter both on land and in the sky.

Prologue

Bzzz.

Though Darren Smith had *finally* fallen asleep, and his phone barely made any noise as it buzzed, he bolted upright in bed, anyway, wide awake in an instant. Everything was blurry as he blinked his eyes, once, twice, and tried to focus on the blinding brightness of the screen so that he could read the text message. It was from his big brother, Ray, and just seeing Ray's name made Darren feel better—for a second, anyway.

D, What's up? Just got your msg. I'm here

Darren had been waiting half the night to hear back from Ray, but he couldn't tell him everything over text.

Darren didn't know exactly what was going on—that was why he had contacted Ray in the middle of the night, after all—but he knew that it was too important for a text message.

v-chat?

logging on now

Darren tucked his phone into his pillowcase and tiptoed out of his bedroom. It was still dark outside, but he glanced out the window, just in case Dad had come home in the night and he'd missed it.

But Dad's space in the driveway was still empty. In the dim glow of the streetlights, Darren could see that only Mom's car was parked there.

In the kitchen, Darren found Mom's laptop on the table. He sneaked a glance over his shoulder, even though he was certain Mom was still asleep. *If only my laptop hadn't melted down . . .* , he thought as he stifled a sigh. Then he would've been able to chat with Ray in his own room—instead of out here, in the open.

Darren flipped up the screen and logged into his v-chat account. To his relief, Ray was already logged on. A warm smile filled Ray's face as Darren opened the screen. Ever since Ray had moved out last year to start college at New Brighton University, Darren had missed him terribly. Not that he would ever admit it aloud—what would be the point? He didn't want Ray to feel bad or anything. Besides, v-chatting was almost as good as getting to hang out with Ray in person.

Almost.

"Little D!" Ray said, his smile widening as he leaned back in his chair. "Sorry I missed your text last night. My psychology midterm is this morning, so I was in the quiet room of the library studying for most of the night. Let's just say my floor mates are pretty much the opposite of quiet."

"The quiet room?" Darren repeated. He and his friend Fiona had been to New Brighton University's library a few times since school had started, but he didn't remember seeing a place called the quiet room.

Ray nodded. "Yeah, it's in the basement—a completely silent place for studying and schoolwork. You're not even allowed to bring in your phone. You have to check it in at the front desk. So I didn't even get your text until, like, four a.m. Otherwise, I would've been right on it. Anyway, what's up?"

Darren got right to the point. "Dad didn't come home last night," he said, lowering his voice. "*Or the night before.*"

A look of surprise flickered across Ray's face for half a second; then it smoothed out, as expressionless as a mask. "Are you sure?" he asked. "Maybe Dad was really busy at work and got home after you were asleep."

Darren shook his head. "I waited up both nights," he said, stifling a yawn. "I mean, it's not like the lab stays open twenty-four hours."

"True," Ray said.

"Besides, he's not even home now," added Darren. "Where would Dad go before six o'clock in the morning? I'm serious, Ray, I really don't think he's been home in"—Darren paused as his throat tightened; he swallowed hard, then continued—"two days."

"Did you ask Mom? What did she say?" Ray wanted to know.

"She won't tell me anything," he said in frustration. "Just like all the times Dad has skipped dinner. She keeps acting like nothing's wrong! Like I'm a little kid who's totally oblivious!"

Ray lifted a finger to his lips, and Darren realized that he was getting kind of loud. A quick glance over his shoulder assured him that Mom was still upstairs.

"Do you think . . . ," Darren began, almost afraid to say the words aloud. He forced himself to say it anyway. "Do you think they're going to get divorced?"

"Divorced? No," Ray said—too quickly. "I mean, yeah, I can see why you might be worried about that. But I'm sure it's not *that* serious. The point is, we don't know anything for sure yet. Maybe Dad's going through, like, a midlife crisis or something."

"You think so?" Darren asked as a note of hope crept into his voice.

"Absolutely," Ray said firmly. "Listen, I'll come home next weekend. We'll talk some sense into them."

Darren liked the sound of that; a weekend hanging out with Ray was just what he needed. Maybe the four of them could do something together—go to a football game or eat dinner at the Willow Cove Café, where Dad had proposed to Mom more than twenty years ago. Maybe that would help Mom and Dad remember what it felt like to be a family.

Just then, Mom's alarm started blaring. It was so loud that even Ray could hear it through their v-chat connection. "I see Mom still needs a foghorn to drag her out of bed," he joked.

"Pretty much," Darren said. "I should go. Mom wouldn't be happy to see me using her laptop."

"Hang in there, D," Ray told him. "And remember, everything's going to work out just fine. It always does."

"Thanks, Ray," replied Darren. "Good luck with your midterm. Talk to you soon."

Then Darren ended their v-chat session. He was about to close Mom's laptop when, all of a sudden, something caught his eye. Mom had left her Internet browser open—and Darren could see the websites she had been looking at before going to bed.

He knew he shouldn't go digging through his mom's stuff. He didn't even mean to look. It was just that the words on the screen—the worst words he'd ever read—jumped out at him before he even had a chance to realize what he was doing.

Jessup, Jessup, & Crumm

DIVORCE ATTORNEYS

Willow Cove · Middletown · New Brighton

Darren's throat felt all tight, as if it were being squeezed by a boa constrictor. All the reassurance he'd felt from his chat with Ray disappeared in an instant. Because if Mom was searching for divorce lawyers, that told Darren everything he needed to know, didn't it?

Almost against his will, Darren's eyes glanced over at the next tab. He didn't think it was possible, but that site was even worse: a whole page of apartment listings in New Brighton. From the map on the screen, Darren could tell they were all just a few blocks away from New Brighton University, where Mom worked as a chemistry professor. Darren remembered, all of a sudden, how much Mom disliked the nearly hour-long commute each way, especially when she was running an experiment late into the night.

Shut it down, Darren told himself, but he wasn't entirely sure if he meant the laptop or his racing thoughts, which were only making him feel worse with every passing second. He closed the computer and bolted away from the kitchen table. It was impossible to believe that just a few minutes ago, Ray was telling him that maybe Mom and Dad could work it out. That maybe everything would be okay.

Now, though, Darren realized that things were so much worse than he could even bear to admit. Sharp, bright sparks crackled down his fingers, but Darren barely noticed them. There was a time, not so long ago, when the truth about himself was the biggest thing on his mind. After all, not every twelve-year-old had to deal with finding out he was actually a Changer: a shapeshifter with the ability to transform into a mythological animal, able to wield stunning and unexpected powers. As an *impundulu* Changer, Darren could transform into a massive bird, control storms, create lightning, and even fly. As the sparks at his fingertips intensified, joining together to create thin, crackling bolts of lightning, Darren's powers were the least of his worries.

For now.

Chapter 1
A NEW MISSION

In a small house across town, Mack Kimura sat across from his grandfather, Jiichan, for breakfast. As usual, Jiichan had prepared a simple Japanese breakfast for them: fluffy steamed rice, scrambled eggs, and a perfectly ripe banana—not to mention two fragrant cups of steaming green tea. But today, there was a big difference. Mack was surprised to also discover a bowl of cornflakes at his place.

"What's this?" he asked. "No anchovies? No porridge? No miso soup?"

Jiichan pretended not to hear him as he lifted a silvery anchovy to his mouth. Mack tried to hide his smile but couldn't quite manage it. For months, Mack and Jiichan had disagreed on just about everything—from what constituted appropriate breakfast foods to Mack's name. Jiichan had insisted on calling him Makoto, while Mack preferred his more American-sounding nickname. Sometimes, it seemed like they couldn't agree on *anything*.

Then, on the first day of school, things had changed forever.

That's when Mack had learned a shocking truth about himself: he wasn't just an average, ordinary kid like he'd always thought. Instead, Mack was a Changer. As a *kitsune*, he had the rare ability to turn himself into a magical fox with a ton of otherworldly powers.

And Mack wasn't alone. A few other kids at Willow Cove Middle School—Gabriella Rivera, Fiona Murphy, and Darren Smith—were Changers too, though each one was a different kind of shape-shifter. In a special class at the end of each school day, they honed their skills and learned how to control their powers—something that was easier said than done. Their teacher, Ms. Dorina Therian, was a werewolf Changer. She was also one of the First

Four, an incredibly powerful group of Changers who have led Changer-kind for more than a thousand years. To Mack's complete amazement, he had discovered that his own grandfather was one of the First Four too. A *kitsune*, like Mack.

At first, Mack thought that Jiichan would be able to tell him exactly how to use his *kitsune* powers. But Jiichan refused, even though Mack was struggling terribly. He knew that Mack needed to figure it out for himself. But when an evil warlock, Auden Ironbound, attacked Willow Cove by using the Horn of Power to control all the adult Changers, it was up to Mack and his friends to stop him. Using their unique powers, Mack, Gabriella, Darren, and Fiona had dealt Auden a serious setback and nearly destroyed the Horn of Power, too, in their first-ever battle. Best of all, Mack and Jiichan had started to understand each other a little better—which made life easier for both of them.

"So, I guess I'll be seeing you in Changers class later," Mack said. "Ms. Therian said that the First Four are coming to class today."

A somber expression settled over Jiichan's wrinkled

face. "Yes," he said. "Makoto, what I am about to say is very important."

Mack shifted uncomfortably in his chair. He could guess what was coming next: a lecture. A few weeks ago, Mack and his friends had directly disobeyed the First Four by going on a secret mission to retrieve a powerful, magical relic, Circe's Compass, from the bottom of the ocean—and the First Four were *not* happy about it. Even though the mission had been, for the most part, a success, there had been even more danger involved when some of Auden Ironbound's followers had attacked Mack and his friends. Luckily, they were able to protect Circe's Compass, but the First Four didn't like being disobeyed.

"You are old enough to understand that trust, once broken, is hard to mend," Jiichan continued. "Though Yara and I believed you capable in retrieving Circe's Compass, Ms. Therian and Sefu were very concerned with how you went off on your own. You broke their trust, but the First Four have collectively deemed it appropriate to assign you another mission."

Mack sat up straighter. That was *not* what he expected Jiichan to say. "But I thought—" he began.

Jiichan held up his hand to quiet Mack; he wasn't done yet. "It is no secret that the First Four are not entirely unified about the best approach to your training," he said. "Yara and I are quite convinced of your abilities. But Sefu . . ."

"Isn't," Mack finished for him.

"That's not what I was going to say," Jiichan replied. "You must learn patience, Makoto. It is as important as anything else I could hope to teach you."

"Sorry," Mack apologized.

"Sefu is worried about the four of you. He fears that your confidence will obscure your judgment. We are well aware that you—all of you—are brave beyond measure," the old man said. "It is only a matter of time before your learned skills match your inherent abilities. What Sefu worries about is the time in between—when you are yet inexperienced in the ways of Changer life; when you are more vulnerable to the dark forces at play in our world."

Mack opened his mouth to argue—he would *never* be vulnerable to Auden Ironbound or his goons; Mack was sure of it—but he caught himself just in time.

"There is no shame in knowing your limits and trusting your allies," Jiichan continued. "It is a sign of strength to ask for help. Even to refuse a mission if it is beyond your capabilities. Do you understand what I am trying to say?"

"Um . . . I think so," Mack said, choosing his words carefully. The truth was, Jiichan's words were almost incomprehensible to him. Say no to a mission? *Not in this lifetime*, Mack thought. He couldn't imagine anything that would stop him from battling Auden Ironbound whenever he had the chance.

From the way his grandfather looked at him, Mack suspected that Jiichan already knew that.

"Know your strengths and your limits, and *never* be afraid to call on an ally when in need," Jiichan said with such a piercing look in his eyes that Mack had to look away.

Luckily for Mack, he heard the rumble of the school bus just then. He shoveled two bites of cornflakes into his mouth as he stood up abruptly. "Gotta go," he said, still not meeting Jiichan's eye. "I'll see you this afternoon, Jiichan."

"Yes," Jiichan said evenly. "Have a good day, Makoto."

When Mack climbed onto the school bus a couple minutes later, his best friend, Joel Hastings, had saved him a seat, like always.

"Did you finish it?" Joel asked impatiently before Mack even had a chance to sit down. "Did you?"

That was all Joel had to say for Mack to know what he was talking about: the latest issue of their favorite comic, Agent Underworld, which had gone on sale just twenty-four hours before.

"Of course I did," Mack replied.

Joel clutched his chest and flopped back against the seat. "Killer, right?" he groaned. "I can't believe they're going to leave us in suspense like that!"

"I can," Mack said with a laugh. "You never know if Agent Underworld is going to survive at the end of each issue. That's how the whole series is written. But trust me, he's going to be just fine. I mean, the series is *named* after him! They're not exactly going to kill him off."

"You don't know that," Joel protested. "What if they *do* kill him off and somebody new becomes Agent Underworld in his place? It won't be the same!"

"That's why they won't kill him off . . . not for real, anyway," Mack pointed out. Still, he had to wonder what Agent Underworld—or any other superhero— would do if he or she ever did meet his or her match. Jiichan's words were still in his mind as he turned to Joel and asked, "What do you think would happen if Agent Underworld didn't have what it takes to battle Captain Corpse?"

Joel blinked. "But you just said—"

"I know, I mean *hypothetically*," Mack cut him off. "Superhero stories are all pretty much the same at their core, right?"

"Actually—" Joel began.

"Hear me out," Mack continued in a rush. "These stories—they're almost always about a hero who pushes himself or herself to the absolute limit and ends up saving the day. But what would happen if a superhero's best wasn't, you know, good enough?"

Joel nodded knowingly. "That's when superhero teams come in," he said.

"You think?" asked Mack.

"Definitely," Joel replied. "Crossovers, superspecials,

that kind of thing. When one hero can't beat an enemy, his friends will always pitch in to help."

"Strength in numbers?" said Mack.

"Exactly," Joel said. "That actually reminds me of how everything went down in Extreme Marauders. . . ."

Joel was still chattering nonstop about Extreme Marauders as the bus pulled up to Willow Cove Middle School. When he noticed Fiona Murphy waiting at Mack's locker, though, Joel gave Mack a nudge. "Nice," he said with a goofy grin on his face.

"Are you serious?" Mack said, shoulder-checking Joel. "Fiona is just my friend, idiot."

"Sure," Joel replied, still grinning. "If you say so." Then he punched Mack in the arm and headed off toward his own locker.

"Hey," Mack said as he approached Fiona.

"Happy Monday," she replied, shifting the heavy stack of books in her arms. Fiona wasn't one to be seen without a few books in hand, but Mack knew why she was lugging them around instead of carrying them in her backpack. Fiona's backpack was where she kept her most precious possession: her *selkie* cloak. Without her cloak, Fiona would lose the ability to transform into a seal. Someone had hidden the cloak from Fiona long ago, when she was just a little baby; after she had found it a few months ago, she vowed to never be separated from it again. Since then, Fiona had been extra gentle with her cloak—she didn't like to cram too many things into her backpack with it.

Thinking about Fiona's *selkie* cloak reminded Mack of something he'd been meaning to ask her. With a quick glance around to make sure no one was close enough to hear their conversation, Mack leaned over to Fiona. "I've been wondering—did the First Four find any *selkies* for you to talk to?"

Fiona sighed. "No, not yet," she replied. "I know they're working on it. The problem is that *selkies* disappear way out to sea for months—even years—at a time. That makes them almost impossible to contact."

Mack let out a low whistle. "So what does that mean for you?" he asked, blunt as always. "You just have to, like, wait? Even though you can't learn any *selkie* songs or powers without them?"

A wry smile crossed Fiona's lips. "Trust me, I'm not just waiting around," she said.

"What do you mean?" Mack asked, a little too eagerly—and a little too loudly.

"I have some leads I'm investigating on my own," she began.

But before Fiona could say more, someone down the hall caught her eye. "Look—it's Darren," she said. She waved her hand awkwardly from beneath her stack of books and called out, "Darren! Hey!"

Darren, though, stared straight ahead as he shuffled down the hall. It was like he couldn't even hear her.

"That's weird," Mack said, scrunching his face into a frown. Darren was nearly about to pass them when Mack reached out and grabbed his arm, jolting Darren out of his thoughts. At the same time, the lights flickered ominously overhead. The usual morning chatter that filled the halls of Willow Cove Middle School went silent as everyone stared upward.

Then, as if nothing had happened, the lights went on again, and the students continued getting ready for homeroom.

"Dude," Mack said in a hushed whisper to Darren, "was that you?"

"Oh—that?" Darren asked, squinting at the lights. "I don't know. Probably. My powers have been acting up a little, but it's no big deal."

"Are you sure?" Mack replied. "I mean, you're making power surges happen just by walking down the hall."

Darren glanced again at the fluorescent lights, which were buzzing steadily once more. "They're fine now," he said, a hint of defensiveness in his voice. "Maybe it wasn't me. Maybe it's just that this dumb school is old and broken."

Fiona and Mack exchanged a glance. That wasn't like Darren, who was one of the most popular kids in school and known for his calm, cool demeanor. But before either could speak, Darren shifted his backpack from one arm to the other. "I've gotta go," he muttered, looking embarrassed. "I don't want to be late for homeroom."

"Of course," Fiona said, stepping aside quickly. Darren's homeroom teacher was superstrict and loved to start the day by giving out a detention or two.

"I'll see you guys later," Darren said. Then he turned and disappeared into the crowd of kids making their way down the hall.

"Well, *that* was weird," Mack said as soon as Darren was out of earshot.

"Something must be bothering him," Fiona agreed.

"But what?" asked Mack. "Our last Changers mission was a success. We didn't even get in trouble. Well—not *that* much trouble, anyway. And it seems like he's having a great football season. The team won their last two games."

"I don't know," Fiona said. "But I hope he tells us soon."

Chapter 2
Disappearances

At lunchtime Fiona searched the cafeteria for Darren, but he was nowhere to be found—which was unusual, since he had so many friends that he was usually right in the middle of a big group of people. *Did he go home sick?* she wondered. He didn't seem sick, though that would explain their strange interaction that morning. Perhaps it was as simple as that.

But when Fiona arrived at the ancillary gym for Changers class that afternoon, she found Mack and Gabriella already transformed into their fox and jaguar forms, respectively, racing on the track—and Darren sitting on the bench, staring into space. Darren was so lost in thought that he didn't even seem to notice when Fiona sat next to him, so close that she could see a blue glow beneath his fingernails.

No sparks, though, she thought. *That's a good sign.*

"Hey," Fiona said, pulling her backpack onto her lap and wrapping her arms around it. "How's everything?"

Darren shrugged, still staring at the far side of the gym. "Fine, I guess," he replied. Then he nodded his head toward the First Four, who were huddled together near the door to the locker rooms. "I forgot they were coming today."

Seriously? Fiona wondered. *It's all Mack's been talking about— How could he forget something like that?* But what she said was, "Mack thinks we're going to get a new mission."

That will have to cheer him up, Fiona thought, watching Darren's face carefully for his reaction.

But Darren didn't respond at all. "As long as they don't want to yell at us," he muttered.

"They weren't *that* upset about the compass," Fiona said. "Besides, we kind of deserved it."

"That's true," admitted Darren. "I'm just sick of people being angry all the time."

"What do you—" Fiona started.

Just then, Ms. Therian clapped her hands loudly; the sound echoed through the ancillary gym. "Everyone, please, gather by the bench; we don't have any time to waste today," she announced.

In a flash Gabriella and Mack changed into their human forms and joined Fiona and Darren on the bench as the First Four crossed the room.

Fiona looked at each one of the First Four—tiny Yara Moreno, an *encantado*, or dolphin Changer, whose face wrinkled up like a walnut as she beamed at the kids. Then there was stern Ms. Therian, a werewolf, whose tough exterior was betrayed by her kind eyes. Sefu Badawi, a *bultungin*, or hyena Changer, looked older than the rest as he leaned heavily on his walking stick. Then, of course, there was Mack's grandfather, Mr. Kimura, a nine-tailed *kitsune*, or fox, Changer. Nine-tailed *kitsunes* were the most powerful of their kind and had incredible abilities. He noticed Fiona looking at him and nodded his head, just once. There was a smile on his face, but something in his eyes—Fiona couldn't quite put her finger on it—gave her pause.

A *warning*, she thought suddenly, then shook her head.

"Before we commence with training today," Ms. Therian said, "we have some urgent information to share with—"

"Don't be alarmed," Yara cut in. "We're not trying to scare you."

As the students exchanged a glance, Ms. Therian shot Yara a look of annoyance.

"Are we in danger?" asked Gabriella.

"If everyone would kindly let me finish," Ms. Therian said pointedly. "Several young Changers in our region have vanished over the last two weeks."

A prickling chill crawled down Fiona's spine as she processed Ms. Therian's words. *Vanished like kidnapped?* she wondered. *Or vanished like disappeared?*

"We believe that the same culprit is responsible for all the abductions," Mr. Kimura spoke up, staring straight at Fiona as though he had read her thoughts.

"'Believe,'" Sefu muttered darkly, "because the truth is, we know nothing for certain."

"Yet!" Yara added, sounding almost chipper. "But that

won't last long. We'll get our younglings back, safe and sound. I'm sure of it."

For a moment Sefu looked like he wanted to argue—but then thought better of it. Instead, a heavy sigh escaped his lips. "Four younglings so far have disappeared from this region—roughly a hundred-mile radius."

"Wait," Fiona cut in. "There are that many young Changers so close to us?"

"I thought Changers were pretty rare," Mack added.

"Unless they have special assignments that take them elsewhere," Sefu began again. "Changers typically live within one hundred miles of a Changer base—in this region, Willow Cove is that base—so there are more of us clustered here."

"Are there Changers classes at other schools, then?" Mack asked. "Can we take a field trip and meet them? Honestly, I'd love to get some inspiration for my comic. . . ."

"There are a few other classes such as ours," Ms. Therian said. "But seeing as there are less than fifteen younglings in the region, and most of them don't attend the same schools, they are usually trained by their families—with the exception of you four, of course. That was the case with most of the kids who have gone missing thus far."

"So ... are *we* in danger?" Gabriella asked, drumming her fingers anxiously on the side of the bench.

"We don't know," Ms. Therian said honestly. "Your guard should be at its highest."

"You must be ever vigilant," Mr. Kimura spoke up.

"Cautious—but not afraid!" Yara added.

Is it just me, or are the First Four totally out of sync today? Fiona thought. She glanced toward Darren, trying to catch his eye. But he was still in his own world.

"We are not telling you this just as a warning," continued Ms. Therian. "Rather, we want to enlist your help in our investigations."

"Yes!" Mack said with a quick fist pump into the air. "So, where do we start?"

"Make no mistake, these will be *our* investigations," Sefu said firmly. "Or to be more precise, Dorina and Akira's investigations. You will be assisting them in their endeavors—*assisting*."

Mack's face fell—but only for a moment. When Yara winked at him and whispered, "Don't mind Sefu. He's just cranky because he missed his nap," the sparkle returned to his eyes.

"The truth is, we know very little about these unusual disappearances," Ms. Therian continued. "The most recent boy to be taken is named Jai. He disappeared last Thursday. He lives with his father in Middletown, and he's a *naga*."

Fiona's hand flew into the air. "What's a *naga*?" she asked. In all her late nights poring over *The Compendium*, an enchanted book all about Changers, she hadn't heard of that type before.

"A serpent Changer," explained Mr. Kimura. "They're originally from India, and only a handful of *naga* live in our region. Jai and his father are two of them."

"Tomorrow after school, Darren and Gabriella will accompany me to Fisherman's Bay National Park," Ms. Therian said.

"I actually have soccer practice tomorrow," Gabriella said. "Coach Connors won't be particularly happy if I skip. I could get a note, though."

"On Wednesday, Mack and Fiona will join me for a trip to Middletown," Mr. Kimura said.

Mack and Fiona exchanged a grin.

"Cool!" Mack cheered. "What will we be investigating?"

"Interviewing," Mr. Kimura corrected him. "We will speak with Jai's father, Ankur. He is deeply distraught about his son's disappearance. This mission is no less important than the other."

Fiona nodded and then looked at Mack. If he was disappointed, he didn't show it.

Ms. Therian turned to the other members of the First Four. "Thank you," she said. "We are always honored to have you join us for class." Then, after Sefu, Yara, and Mr. Kimura left, she addressed the students.

"Now, let's start our drills," Ms. Therian continued. "Fiona, you'll be practicing your underwater breathing exercises. I'd like you to manage thirty minutes underwater by the end of the month, so you've got a lot of work to do. Gabriella and Mack—hurdles for you."

"Hurdles?" Mack asked, perking up immediately. "That's different."

"That won't be necessary," said Ms. Therian. "

rather not attract any attention for out-of-the-ordin

behavior. We'll leave directly after your practice a

drive to the park—that's where Jai was last seen. Th

we can search for any clues that the abductors mi

have left behind."

"Like footprints? Or, uh, broken branches?" M:

asked, sounding a little wistful. It was obvious that

wanted to go on the mission, too.

"Yes—and also traces of magic," Ms. Therian s:

"It's a rare warlock who can use magic without leav:

at least some sign of it behind. Too subtle for hun

senses, of course, but that's where our abilities will

of great use. It also helps to know where to look, so

teach you the signs to watch for, as well."

Mack could barely contain his disappointment, l

under his grandfather's steady gaze, he didn't compla

Fiona understood how he felt. She kind of wished t!

she had been chosen for the trip to Fisherman's I

too. *I guess there's not much a seal can do in the forest,* s

thought, but being practical about it didn't make l

feel any better.

Ms. Therian didn't smile, but Fiona definitely caught a twinkle in her dark eyes. "As I believe your grandfather sometimes says, Mack, life's not all about the race."

Then Ms. Therian turned to Darren. "And for you, Darren . . . target practice."

She gestured to the far side of the ancillary gym, where targets of various sizes had been carefully arranged. "Your goal is perfect accuracy, which shouldn't be hard given the *impundulu*'s extraordinarily keen eyesight. Since today is your first time, though, I'll settle for your best."

Ms. Therian glanced at Fiona, Mack, Gabriella, and Darren, one by one. Then she nodded her head. That was their cue, Fiona knew, to transform. As she bent over to unzip her backpack for her *selkie* cloak, she missed the rapid flashes as her friends changed into their animal forms.

With the soft, gray *selkie* cloak in her hands, Fiona hurried over to the saltwater pool. She slipped the cloak over her shoulders; though it was almost weightless in her hands, she felt a familiar heaviness settle over her. Then Fiona twirled, just once . . .

It was as easy as that.

In her sleek seal form, Fiona plunged into the salt-water pool. She flicked her tail and zipped through the water, almost laughing with delight. It wasn't like swimming in the ocean—nothing could be that glorious, that wild and free—but it was a pretty good substitute. In the water, Fiona could lose herself, becoming a seal so fully that she forgot about everything else around her.

Not today, though.

Even underwater, where sound and light were distorted, Fiona was aware of a commotion in the ancillary gym. *Focus*, she reminded herself, picturing the oxygen in her lungs lasting longer than ever before as the seconds stretched into minutes. She'd love to break her record from last week, when she'd somehow managed to spend almost twenty-seven minutes submerged.

But those voices—they were getting louder. Fiona tilted her head, hoping to hear more clearly; it was so odd that she could hear sounds underwater from miles away, but noise from above was just a jumble. At last, Fiona's curiosity got the better of her, and she propelled herself up to the surface of the water . . . in time to see one of

Darren's lightning bolts hit a massive windowpane near the ceiling. It shattered in an explosion of sparks and glittering glass, and shards rained down into the far end of the pool, pelting the water like hard pieces of hail.

The gym was very quiet—almost unbearably still—for about half a second.

Then a blast from Ms. Therian's whistle pierced the air.

Uh-oh, Fiona thought. Ms. Therian only used her whistle like that when things were bad.

And from the look on her face, they were about to get worse.

"Get out of the pool, Fiona," Ms. Therian barked.

Fiona scrambled out of her cloak and up the ladder. When Ms. Therian sounded like that, she wasn't messing around. *What's going on?* Fiona wondered, blinking her dark blue eyes. She hoped practice wasn't about to be cut short. The chance to change into her *selkie* form was the highlight of her day, and Fiona didn't want to miss a minute of it.

"Darren to the bench!" Ms. Therian yelled as she strode across the floor.

The great bird soared down to the floor; a moment

later, Darren was back in his human form. He hung his head in shame as he braced himself for Ms. Therian's lecture.

"I'm terribly confused," she began, her voice like ice. "Your powers at our last meeting were finely tuned, yet today, you have missed every target. The only thing left to conclude is that you are either distracted or careless. And a Changer's carelessness can bear terrible consequences. I don't think I need to tell you that the pool is right below the window you shattered. We are lucky Fiona was training at the other end."

"I know," Darren said miserably. "I'm sorry. It just— it just got away from me."

"But it *cannot* get away from you—ever," Ms. Therian said. "That is why we meet here each day. So that you can master your powers. So that *you* can control *them*."

Darren, too upset to speak, simply nodded.

"There are ten more minutes until the bell," Ms. Therian said with a sigh. "Darren, I want you on the bench for the rest of the class—try to meditate, and bring that focus to practice tomorrow. You too, Fiona. The pool is off-limits until it's been cleaned."

Fiona tried to stifle her disappointment as she reached for a towel. *At least now I can go talk to Darren,* she thought. Whatever was bothering him was clearly still on his mind. And it was obvious that Fiona wasn't the only one who was concerned. Over by the track, Gabriella's gold *nahual* eyes glimmered with sympathy as she watched Darren trudge over to the bench. *She must know how he feels,* Fiona realized. After all, it wasn't so long ago that Gabriella's transformations had been unpredictable too.

After Fiona dried off, she joined Darren on the bench. "Hey," she began.

"I'm really sorry," he said, his voice strangely flat. "You have to know that was a complete accident."

"Of course I know that," Fiona replied at once.

"And I ruined your Changers class, too," he continued, his head in his hands. "I'm ruining everything."

"No," Fiona said. "Don't say that. It was just one mistake."

"I don't want to hurt anyone," Darren said. "I just want..."

Darren's voice trailed off as his phone started to

buzz. He rummaged around in his backpack until he found it. Fiona glanced over her shoulder nervously at Ms. Therian, who was coaching Mack and Gabriella through their last drill. If Darren was caught on his phone—even at the end of class—he'd be in more trouble.

"My brother texted me," he said.

Fiona watched his face as Darren read the text. Somehow, he looked even more upset when he finished it. "What happened? What's wrong?" she asked. "Is Ray okay?"

Darren shook his head. "I—I have to go," he said, standing so abruptly that he knocked his backpack off the bench. At the same moment the lights in the ancillary gym blazed brighter than the sun. There was a sudden, earsplitting pop—

And every bulb burned out.

"Darren—" Fiona called.

But her voice was drowned out by the final bell, and Darren was already gone.

When Fiona got home from school that afternoon, she grabbed her journal and went straight to her favorite spot on the beach, Broad Rock. Her father, who had no clue that Fiona was really a *selkie*, had forbidden her from swimming alone, claiming it was too dangerous. That was true for a human, of course. But a *selkie* was safest in the ocean, Fiona was sure about that.

Fiona didn't like to break the rules, though, so instead of putting on her *selkie* cloak for a quick swim in the churning ocean, she simply perched on Broad Rock, her backpack on her lap and her journal in her hands. Fiona didn't even bother opening her journal. While she loved writing in it before going to bed every night, when she brought it to the beach, it was nothing more than a prop. Because the real reason Fiona came to the shore every day, rain or shine, was to find the copper-colored seal.

She'd only seen the seal twice before—once when she'd found her *selkie* cloak, buried in the damp sand below Broad Rock, and once during the battle against Auden Ironbound—but Fiona was as sure as she could be that it was no ordinary animal. The unusual sheen to its coat and its brightly inquisitive eyes told Fiona there was something more there. Fiona was too rational to jump to conclusions, though; she wanted proof before she told anyone else.

But when she was very quiet, and listened to her heart, Fiona knew that the copper-colored seal was a *selkie*.

And if Fiona was right, then this was the *selkie* she'd been searching for. The one who could teach her the songs and tell her their secrets. The one who could help Fiona unlock all the powers that she didn't even know she had.

I'm here, Fiona sent a message across the wide expanse of the ocean, somehow wishing that her thoughts could carry through the waves and reach the *selkie*; call her to shore. *Please come. I need you.*

The only response, though, was the gentle lapping of waves as they washed onto the sand. Fiona didn't mind—not really, anyway. She was patient. Besides, next to being in the water, this little spot was Fiona's favorite place in the whole world.

As the sun began to set, making the ocean glitter like it was made of sapphires and diamonds, Fiona suddenly felt a hand on her back. She was so startled that she jumped and spun around, accidentally knocking her backpack from her lap. But it was only her father.

"Dad," Fiona said as a relieved smile filled her face.

"I thought I'd find you here," Dad replied, smiling back. "Sometimes it seems like you spend all your free time down at the shore."

"Can you blame me?" Fiona asked as she stared at the sunset. The golden sun shimmered as it dipped beyond the horizon, bathing the sky with shades of crimson and violet.

"You've always been my water baby, Fee," Dad said, using her special nickname. "Even during a cold rain I couldn't stop you from jumping into puddles."

They both smiled. Fiona barely remembered her mother, who had died when she was a toddler. Sometimes Fiona could reach down deep to recall snippets of the songs she sung or the way her mother's cotton dresses smelled, but her father had always been there for her. His students at New Brighton University didn't think he was very warm or friendly, but Fiona knew the truth: Dad had a soft side, and he loved her as much as she loved him.

"Come on, let's go make dinner," Dad said as he bent

over to pick up Fiona's backpack. "This got all sandy," he continued, brushing it off. "I'll wash it for you tonight so it will be dry by morning."

"No!" Fiona cried, grabbing her backpack away from him.

She knew at once that she'd messed up. A look of concern—with just a touch of suspicion—crossed her dad's face. I *have to fix this*, Fiona thought.

"You already do, like, *everything*," she said. "I can wash my own backpack. Seriously. I want to help more."

There was a pause before Dad spoke. Then he wrapped his arm across Fiona's shoulders and pulled her in for a hug. "You're such a great kid," he said. "What did I do to deserve you?"

"What did I do to deserve *you*?" Fiona countered as she stood on tiptoe to kiss her dad's cheek. But inside, she felt . . . well . . . like a liar. *If he only knew,* she thought.

But of course, that was impossible.

If Dad ever found out that she was a *selkie* . . .

It would be disastrous.

Chapter 3
THE STORM

Sure enough, when Darren got home from school, Ray was waiting in the living room—just like he'd texted. Darren dropped his stuff and got right to the point. "I thought you said you couldn't come home until next weekend," he said. What was wrong with his voice? Why did it sound so accusatory? Ray, of all people, hadn't done anything wrong. Darren tried to take a deep breath, tried to steady himself, but that jumpy, jittery feeling was still going strong.

Luckily, Ray didn't seem to take offense as he crossed the room and pulled Darren into a bear hug. "That was my plan," he said. "But Mom showed up after my midterm and said we needed to have a family meeting. So here I am."

"This is weird," Darren said anxiously. "Very weird."

Even the happiness of seeing Ray wasn't enough to eliminate the feeling of dread that weighed on Darren's heart. But Ray was here, at least. Whatever was about to happen, Darren knew that he wouldn't be facing it alone.

Just then, Mom came in from the kitchen. "Darren!" she said. "I didn't hear you come in."

"What's going on?" Darren asked.

"Let's all sit," Mom said carefully, avoiding his question. She called over her shoulder, "Alan? He's home."

Dad's back, Darren realized with a sudden rush of relief. He hadn't seen or even heard from his father since Saturday morning. But now, here they were, the whole family together again. That was a start. A good start.

"Hey, buddy," Dad said as he crossed the room and gave Darren a quick hug. Dad smiled, but it didn't completely reach his eyes.

"Dad," Darren said. "Where have you been? I haven't seen you in—"

Dad patted Darren's back. "We're going to talk about that," he said. "We're going to talk about everything."

"Come on, D," Ray said from the love seat by the picture window. "Sit with me."

Darren crossed the room and sat next to Ray. His legs were jumping—it was like his knees were rattling in their sockets—so he pressed his palms on them, hard, to make them stop.

Mom and Dad sat too at opposite ends of the couch. Mom's shoulders were so tense, so high. That feeling of dread surged through Darren again, but he tried to quash it. *You don't know anything*, he told himself. *Stop freaking out.*

For a long moment no one spoke. Mom and Dad exchanged a glance, but what they were communicating between themselves, Darren couldn't tell. Then Mom took a deep breath.

"This isn't a conversation we ever wanted to have with you," Mom began. "It's— I—"

As her voice faltered, Dad sighed. "What your mother is trying to say," he began, "is . . ."

"We've decided to get a divorce," Mom finished.

No one moved.

That's it, Darren thought numbly, staring into the great empty space between his parents. His worst fear—the worry that had been gnawing at him for months—was actually happening. It hadn't sank in yet, that big, awful word. "Divorce."

But it was real, and it was happening—like it or not.

"Why?" Darren asked, and his voice sounded all thin and small, like he was still a little kid. Darren cleared his throat and tried again. "Why?"

"Oh, baby," Mom said, dabbing her eyes. She held her arms open wide. "Come here."

But Darren didn't budge.

"There isn't one specific reason," Dad said. "We've just grown apart. We've been married for twenty-three years, you know. That's a long time."

"Yeah," Ray said, a hard edge to his voice. "A *really* long time. It sure seems like a shame to throw away a marriage like that. A family like this."

"We're not throwing away our family," Mom protested. "But we can't go on like we have. All this fighting and discord—it's not healthy for anyone."

"Well, maybe if *you* were here more," Ray snapped, turning to Dad. "I mean, come on—you didn't even come home for two nights?"

"Ray. Calm down. I asked Dad to leave," Mom said evenly.

"What about all the times he missed dinner to work late? Or hang out with his buddies instead of putting his *family* first?" Ray demanded.

Dad took a deep breath; Darren could tell he was trying to stay calm. "Son, I'm not a perfect person," Dad told him. "I've made mistakes—I'll be the first one to admit that. But to be honest with you, your mother and I have not been happy together for a while. Sometimes the best thing for me to do was clear out. To give us both a little space."

"And that's when we realized that we're actually happier apart," Mom spoke up. "This isn't some spur-of-the-moment decision, you know. We've been thinking and talking about it for a long time. And we can't keep denying it—Dad and I aren't in love with each other anymore, and we don't want to stay married."

"So what now?" asked Ray. "I mean, what happens

next? Exactly what does it look like when the Smiths Get Divorced?"

Mom ignored Ray's sarcasm, even though she'd never tolerated one word of back talk before. "We filed for divorce last week," she explained. "The process will take several months to finalize."

"What does that mean for Darren?" said Ray. "Where's he going to live?"

"With me," said Mom, glancing at Dad out of the corner of her eye. "At least, until custody decisions are finalized."

Custody.

The word made Darren feel like throwing up.

"And where's Dad going to go, now that you're throwing him out?" Ray asked.

"Okay, son, that's enough," Dad said, a hint of warning in his voice. "That's your mother you're talking to. She deserves your respect."

"Sorry," Ray mumbled. "But this is a lot to take in."

"To answer your question, Mom's not 'throwing me out,'" Dad said. "I found an apartment right here in Willow Cove—it's a pretty good place—and I'll be moving out next weekend. But, Darren, don't worry, buddy, you'll still see me all the time . . . every other weekend, and sometimes longer for holidays and school breaks."

"All the time"? Darren thought. *That doesn't sound like "all the time" to me. It sounds more like "hardly ever."*

"And, Ray—whenever you want to hang out, my door is open," Dad continued. "You'll have your own key and everything."

"Darren, baby," Mom tried again. "You've been so quiet. Are you all right? Is there anything you want to ask us?"

Darren pressed his lips together tightly. The truth was, he had about a million questions—starting with why Mom was searching for apartment listings in New Brighton on her laptop. But even more urgent than his questions was the fear hammering away inside his heart. His fists were clenched, but not just because he was angry; Darren could feel that familiar crackle snapping through his fingers. Right now, he could barely control his emotions, let alone his powers. Everything in his world seemed uncertain, upside down. There was only one thing Darren knew for sure: he had to get out of there.

"May I be excused?" he asked quietly.

Mom and Dad exchanged another glance. "Sure," Mom said. "We're here for you whenever you want to talk, honey."

Of course you are—except when Dad leaves, or you're backed up at work, or you don't feel like it, Darren thought as his anger got the better of him.

As he hurried from the living room and charged up the stairs, he could hear Ray. "Look how upset he is," Ray was saying. "You couldn't have held it together for a few more years, until he goes to college? I sure hope you're happy. Since your happiness seems to matter more than anyone else's."

Before Mom or Dad could reply, Darren was in his bedroom. He slammed the door—harder than he meant to—and flipped on the light. Then Darren leaned against the door so that no one could come in and, at last, exhaled, a jagged breath that made his chest ache. In a matter of moments, his whole world had cracked wide open, and it hurt worse than he ever could've imagined.

It's not that the news was a surprise. The joke, Darren thought bitterly, was that he had been in denial for such a long time. *Stupid,* he thought. *You saw all the signs and you still pretended—you still hoped—*

Darren's thoughts were all-consuming, but somewhere in his consciousness he became aware of a dull buzzing noise, like the sound of bees swarming on a summer's day. His palms were warm—uncomfortably warm—and between the heat and the noise, it was enough to pull Darren from his thoughts. He stared down at his hands, which glowed with pulsing electricity. Darren blinked and looked again, but the glow was only more intense. And it was spreading.

He yanked up his sleeves, and his mouth dropped open in astonishment. Crackling bolts of electricity were racing up his veins, illuminating them beneath his skin.

Nothing like this had ever happened before.

The lights overhead flickered ominously.

You've gotta get ahold of your powers, Darren scolded himself. He was losing control—it was slipping farther and farther out of reach with every passing second as his emotions surged, threatening to overwhelm him and everything else.

With Ms. Therian's warning ringing in his head, Darren remembered the breathing exercises Gabriella always did when her *nahual* powers started to break through. *Ten . . . nine . . . eight . . .* , he thought.

There was a knock at the door.

No, Darren thought anxiously. *Get out of here!* He wasn't even close to regaining control.

"D, it's me." Ray's voice, low and comforting, floated through the closed door. "Can I come in?"

In his heart Darren wanted nothing more than to see Ray—Ray, who knew exactly how he felt; Ray, who would understand everything. But the electrical currents were still racing up his arms and growing stronger—

"I—I just want to be alone," Darren said in a strangled voice. "Can we—can we talk tomorrow?"

On the other side of the door, Ray was quiet for a long moment. In the silence, Darren could hear something besides the thrum of electricity under his skin: a long, low rumble of thunder.

"Whatever you want, buddy," Ray finally said. "I'm here for you. Any time."

"Thanks," Darren said gratefully. But when he heard Ray's footsteps retreating down the stairs, he felt even worse. No one at school—not even his Changer friends—could understand the kind of pain Darren felt. Only Ray could, and by sending him away, Darren knew he was truly alone. The thought made his hands burn even hotter.

Boom!

The house shuddered from the sound of the thunder; the storm was moving fast. The lights flickered repeatedly; with mounting horror, Darren realized that they were flickering in unison with his hands. Then suddenly, Darren heard the pounding of rain on the roof.

The storm had arrived.

And it was calling him, pulling him toward the window. Darren found himself moving across the room, throwing sparks with every motion. He yanked back the curtains and shoved the window open.

The blast of cool air felt good on his burning skin. Overhead, the billowing clouds churned, as wild as the ocean during a hurricane. Bolts of lightning glimmered and crackled—two, three, ten at a time. Darren had never seen anything like it, and even through his anguish he could acknowledge its beauty. He held his hands in the air and watched them crackle with lightning, pulsing in time with the massive bolts overhead.

It's me, he realized. *I've caused this storm.*

His powers . . . They were greater than Darren had ever dreamed. As the lights went out, plunging the entire street into darkness, a terrible realization dawned on him. *What will I do if I can't get control?* he wondered. *What will happen if Mom and I move to New Brighton, away from my friends and Ms. Therian and the First Four?*

How will I ever learn to control my powers without them?

Chapter 4
FISHERMAN'S BAY

At lunch the next day, Gabriella joined her soccer friends. "What's up?" she asked the other girls, who were clustered around Josie's cell phone.

Trisha, the team captain, glanced up. "You have *got* to see this video," she said. "Did you hear the big storm last night?"

Gabriella nodded. "Definitely—the power went out, and I couldn't finish blow-drying my hair. You know how miserable it is to sleep with wet hair?"

Trisha grimaced sympathetically. "That's the worst," she replied. "The storm was *really* bad. When you see Josie's video, you'll totally understand why we all lost power."

Gabriella leaned in close as Josie played the video again. At first the video was pretty unremarkable. Sure, it was a big storm, but Willow Cove was close enough to the ocean that strong rainstorms were pretty frequent.

As the storm grew, though, Gabriella found herself captivated by the video. There was so much lightning that the dense wall of clouds seemed to glow from within.

"Just wait until the lightning *really* gets going," Josie said. "In five, four, three, two—"

Crack!

"That house!" Gabriella exclaimed as a massive bolt of lightning ripped through the sky. It almost made a direct hit—

"Wait for it," said Josie.

Then the clouds seemed to explode as another enormous bolt suddenly scattered into a swirling fireball of sparks. Gabriella's breath caught in her throat as it happened again: all those blazing sparks pulled together into a thick bolt that came perilously close to hitting the same house again and again.

And again.

And again.

"Crazy, right?" Trisha's voice cut through Gabriella's thoughts. "I've never seen lightning do that before."

"Yeah," Gabriella managed to say.

"You should put it online," Lauren told Josie.

"Ooh, great idea," Josie said, and she uploaded the video. "Do you think it will go viral?"

"It might," Abby replied. "And speaking of going viral, did you see Crash Course's new video?"

As her friends began chatting excitedly about their favorite band's latest release, Gabriella tuned them out. Her mind was whirling with thoughts—about the storm, the lightning, and what, exactly, was at the center of it all. No one else had seemed to notice that the house directly beneath the storm and all those strange lightning bolts belonged to someone they all knew.

It was where Darren lived.

Gabriella was still thinking about the video as she walked across the parking lot after soccer practice to meet Ms. Therian and Darren. Obviously, Darren would've been aware of the storm—it was happening literally above his house—but had he caused it? And if so, did he even realize it? Gabriella had struggled so hard to keep her *nahual* powers under control; to be honest, she was still struggling, but weekly coaching from Gabriella's aunt, Tía Rosa, was helping a lot. She knew, though, that she'd never forget the dread and hopelessness she felt when her powers overcame her against her will. *If Darren's going through that, I have to talk to him,* she thought. Gabriella didn't want him to feel as alone as she had before her aunt started helping her.

Then she shook her head. *But what if he thinks I'm accusing him of causing the storm?* she thought. *Or, worse, he thinks I'm saying he can't handle his powers?*

Then Gabriella thought about Darren's performance in Changers class that afternoon, which had been disastrous again. For a moment Gabriella had wondered if Ms. Therian would still let him go on their mission this afternoon. Gabriella had learned the hard way that her own powers were even more difficult to control when her emotions were running high. Could the same thing be happening for Darren?

When Gabriella reached Ms. Therian's car, Darren and Ms. Therian were already there. *I'll have to wait until*

Darren and I are alone to talk to him, Gabriella thought. The last thing she wanted was to get him in more trouble with Ms. Therian.

"Excellent," Ms. Therian said as Gabriella jogged over to them. "Into the car. I'll brief you both on the way."

After everyone put on their seat belts, Ms. Therian pulled out of the parking lot. "As I told you yesterday, Jai disappeared the previous Thursday," she began. "He was last seen by his father that afternoon. Apparently, Jai met up with some friends to ride his bike through the park, which they did until about thirty minutes before sunset, when they split up for the day. Jai said he was going home but never arrived. His bike was found abandoned on the trail the next morning."

Gabriella closed her eyes and pictured it: the fading light, the dead leaves crunching underfoot, the boy who never made it home. She shivered with a sudden, unspeakable fear. "How long has Jai known he was a Changer?" she asked.

"A few months," Ms. Therian replied. "He is unusually skilled. In fact, he came into his powers earlier than expected. He's just eleven."

"But I thought Changer powers didn't show up until their twelfth birthday," Darren spoke up.

"That is almost always the case," said Ms. Therian. "But it has been known to happen—especially when one has been born with exceptionally strong powers. Of course, it is not just that the powers show up early. They tend to reveal themselves in an unusually dramatic way."

That got Gabriella's attention. "Did that happen with Jai?" she asked.

Ms. Therian sighed. "It did," she said. "*Naga* wield control over water and weather, among other powers. Jai did not mean to, of course, but he caused a terrible flood in Middletown."

"I remember that!" Gabriella exclaimed. "They said it was the worst flood in two hundred years!"

"So it was," Ms. Therian said grimly.

"He must have been so scared," Gabriella said. "Do you think he reached out for help? Like, to someone who's not a Changer? Someone who might've kidnapped him?"

"I highly doubt it," Ms. Therian replied. "Remember,

his father is a Changer too, so when it became clear that Jai had caused the flood, he was able to intervene and begin his training. Though I suppose it is possible Jai told a non-Changer. There is still much surrounding Jai's disappearance that we don't yet know."

"Speaking of stuff you don't know," Darren began, "how did you miss him? I thought there was this whole network of Changers dedicated to finding new Changers *before* their powers appeared."

Gabriella blinked in surprise at Darren's tone of voice. He was always so friendly, so easygoing. But lately, more often than not, he sounded upset—even angry. *Something is definitely going on with him,* she thought.

But if Ms. Therian was bothered by Darren's rudeness, she didn't show it. "Yes, you are correct," she said. "But the system is far from perfect. Occasionally, a youngling coming into his or her powers slips by, undetected, which is what happened with Jai. Even though his father is a Changer, we never expected Jai's powers to appear so early."

"I guess that's like life," Darren replied, staring out the window. "It never quite works out like you expect."

As the car approached Fisherman's Bay National Park, the road narrowed; the forest grew more dense. Gabriella tried to catch Darren's eye, but he was turned away from her—and he never looked over, not even once.

"We will begin by retracing Jai's last known movements," Ms. Therian said as she parked the car. "We don't have a lot of time before sunset, so we will need to move quickly."

"What are we looking for, exactly?" asked Darren.

"Anything suspicious, really," Ms. Therian said. "Anything that seems out of place. Most of all, I want you to listen to your intuition. If something feels off— or wrong in any way—I expect you to speak up."

"Is that how we'd know if magic was used?" asked Gabriella. "Our . . . intuition?"

Ms. Therian nodded. "You'll feel it before you have the ability to see it," she explained.

Darren perked up a little. "See it? Like, *see* actual signs of magic with our eyes?"

"What does it look like?" asked Gabriella.

"It is difficult to describe," Ms. Therian said thoughtfully. "For me, it is the hint of a shimmer, a gleam that you barely see from the corner of your eye before it disappears . . . like a memory of something that was there but is no more."

For a few minutes no one spoke as they walked along the trail. Soon, it forked into two separate paths.

"Which one did Jai take?" asked Gabriella.

Ms. Therian paused and closed her eyes. "Both," she finally said. "I believe he took both. I will take the right trail; you two take the left. The paths meet up again after about a hundred yards, near the entrance to the bay. Shout if you find anything, and I will be right there."

Gabriella could hardly believe that Ms. Therian was going to let her and Darren investigate on their own—especially after all the warnings the First Four had given them in Changers class yesterday—but the sun was set-ting pretty quickly. Maybe it was just in the interest of time. Either way, Ms. Therian was already disappearing into the trees, her footsteps crackling over the carpet of fallen leaves.

This is perfect, Gabriella thought. *Now that we have a few minutes by ourselves, maybe Darren will tell me what's going on.*

"You coming?" Darren asked. Their side of the trail narrowed even further, so that the spruce branches on either side created a canopy overhead. Darren pushed one of the branches and held it out of the way for Gabriella.

"Thanks," she said, hurrying to catch up. "Listen, I've been meaning to talk to you about something."

"Sounds serious," Darren replied. "Anything wrong?"

"That's what I wanted to ask you," continued Gabriella. "What's going on?"

Darren shrugged, but he wouldn't meet her eye. "I— Nothing, really. School, Changers stuff, football practice. Same old, same old."

A hint of a frown flickered over Gabriella's face. *He's not getting off the hook that easily,* she thought.

"Are you sure?" she asked lightly. "Because you've seemed pretty . . . I don't know, *upset* for the last couple days."

Darren's laugh was tense. "I don't know what makes you think that," he said. "Trust me, everything's fine. I just have a lot of stuff going on right now."

"I think it might be more than that," Gabriella said,

fishing around in her pocket for her phone. "The girls showed me this at lunch earlier."

Darren's expression was part confusion, part intrigue as he walked over to Gabriella. "What's this?" he asked as the video loaded.

"Maybe you can tell me," she said.

A sudden realization dawned on him. "That's my house!" he exclaimed as the clouds gathered over it, blazing with lightning.

"One of my friends took this video during the storm yesterday. But it wasn't an ordinary storm, was it?"

At last, Darren looked directly into Gabriella's eyes. What she saw there—a sea of swirling emotions; fear and anger and guilt and sadness all jumbled up, each more intense than the last—was so familiar.

But all too soon, Darren broke her gaze. He turned abruptly and began walking down the path away from Gabriella, her phone, and the video that proved all of Gabriella's worries.

Wait, Gabriella thought. It wasn't supposed to happen like this. "Please, Darren, I want to help," she urged him.

"You wouldn't understand," he said, walking faster with his fists balled up.

"You don't know that," Gabriella shot back, lowering her voice as she noticed a couple of teenagers—a boy and a girl—ahead of them on the trail. "Would you just *try* to trust me? I've been there—I've had my powers surge out of my control. I know what you're going through—"

"You don't know *anything* about what I'm going through!" Darren exploded. At the same moment a white-hot bolt of lightning burst from his fingertips— right in the direction of the teenagers on the path.

"Duck!" Gabriella screamed at the top of her voice.

Oddly enough, though, they didn't need to.

It all happened so fast: the air wavering as some unseen force—a shield or something—surrounded the teens, who stared through it with empty black eyes at Darren and Gabriella.

It was magic.

But where had it come from?

Then Darren grabbed her arm. "That's—that's— He's a warlock," he gasped. "Bram, remember? I saw him at New Brighton University—and then he was on the beach, when we tried to get Circe's Compass."

Gabriella stretched and flexed her muscles, like she did just before practice. She wanted desperately to transform, but she didn't want to start a fight. After all, maybe the teenagers would flee—report back to whomever they worked for.

That was never going to happen, though. The shimmering shield began to fade, disintegrating before their eyes, and Gabriella understood at last what Ms. Therian meant about sensing the reminder of where magic once had been.

The witch's hands were clenched tightly together, and her dark lips were moving with silent words—

It's a curse, Gabriella realized as she dodged the spell just in time.

Zzzzap! One of Darren's lightning bolts cut through the air, but it missed the witch by several feet.

In an instant Gabriella changed into her *nahual* form and jumped in front of Darren. A low, menacing growl rumbled in her throat.

As another curse zinged past Gabriella, she stood her

ground, the velvety black fur bristling along the back of her neck. When the moment was right, she would pounce. She would have to take them both out with one tackle; if she tried to attack them separately, there would still be one left to curse her.

Unless Darren's lightning..., she thought suddenly.

Darren, in his human form, responded, *You got it, Gabriella. You take her out. I'll block him.*

Gabriella watched in amazement as one of Darren's lightning bolts intercepted a curse, causing it to sizzle up into a puff of smoke. A brief smile of relief flickered across his face—but it didn't last. It soon became clear that Darren's strike was a lucky one, because each bolt of lightning after that was increasingly unpredictable. They ricocheted through the air, slicing through leaves, singeing tree trunks. Thin plumes of smoke spiraled into the sky, the smell of char thick in the air.

Darren! Watch out! Gabriella thought to him desperately. Even with her heightened *nahual* senses, she didn't know how she could manage to keep track of both the magic-users *and* Darren's wild lightning. The problem was that Darren's lightning was just as dangerous as the real thing. A thick bolt, crackling with even more power than the others, shot straight into the air—and sliced off a heavy branch from the pine tree above Gabriella. It fell in an instant, pinning her to the forest floor.

I *can't move!* Gabriella cried out to Darren as she struggled beneath the branch.

I'*m sorry!* Darren responded, and Gabriella could feel his desperation. I'*m trying*—I'*m trying my best*—

But right now, Darren's best wasn't good enough. With a malicious gleam in her eye, the witch began to cast a new curse.

Darren! Gabriella screamed.

A lightning bolt burst from his hands instantaneously...

And zoomed straight toward Gabriella.

Chapter 5
THE WRISTBAND

"No!" Darren howled, seeing what was about to happen and entirely powerless to prevent it.

Gabriella strained against the fallen branch, but even though she tried her hardest to move it, she couldn't get out of the way in time.

The lightning bolt found its mark, and suddenly, Gabriella lay very still. The thick, choking smell of singed fur filled the air, and Darren fell to his knees, overwhelmed with guilt.

A streak of steel gray bounded past him then, shoving Darren out of the way. He landed so hard that the air was knocked out of his lungs; gasping, he looked up and saw Ms. Therian in her werewolf form.

Their teacher was imposing as a human, but as a werewolf, she was downright terrifying. Her long, razor-sharp teeth couldn't be contained in her mouth, which was open in a perpetual snarl; there was a brutality to her every movement that made Darren feel afraid, even though he felt safer with her than just about anyone else in the world.

And if *he* felt afraid, the witch and warlock must have been really terrified. Ms. Therian only had to lunge at them once and they were off, running for their lives through the thick brush, not even bothering to send any curses flying back at the Changers. Ms. Therian continued to chase them, anyway.

"Gabriella!" Darren gasped, scrambling to his feet. He raced across the clearing to her. Somehow, she was back in her human form, and her face was very pale; with her help, Darren rolled the branch out of the way. "Are you okay? Please say something! Please!"

It seemed to take a lot of effort, but eventually she smiled. "I'm good," she managed to choke out. "A little sore, but okay."

"The lightning," Darren said, biting his lip. "I thought it hit—"

"It did," she interrupted him in a quiet voice. "Just the edge of my ear, though."

Darren looked closer and saw a bright red burn on the edge of her ear. "I'm so sorry," he said miserably. "I would never, never, *never*—"

"You don't need to explain that," Gabriella told him. "I told you, I've been through the whole out-of-control powers thing. You can trust me—just tell me what's going on."

Darren squeezed his eyes shut tight, trying to hold back the tears that had suddenly filled them.

"Hey," Gabriella said, reaching out to pat his arm. "Look, everything's going to be okay—"

"It's *not*," he said through clenched teeth. "I could've gotten us both killed! I can't fight, I can't control my lightning, I am *failing* at everything important, at everything that *matters*."

"No—"

"I can't do it, Gabriella," he continued. "I don't know how to get control."

"I didn't know how to either . . . ," she began, but at that moment, Ms. Therian rejoined them. She was back in her human form, without a single hair out of place from the long, silver-streaked braid that fell heavily down her back.

"Gracious," she said, bending down to examine Gabriella. "Tell me everything. What *happened?*"

A long look passed between Gabriella and Darren, and he had the sudden feeling that she was going to tell Ms. Therian everything, including how Darren's initial outburst caused him to fling lightning at two people unintentionally. *If they hadn't been magic and blocked the bolt, I don't know what would've happened. . . . Please don't tell, Gabriella, he begged. Please don't.*

"They must've sensed we were Changers," Gabriella said, choosing her words carefully. "All of a sudden, they attacked. There was, like, no warning."

"None," Darren agreed, feeling a rush of gratitude toward his friend.

A pensive frown crossed Ms. Therian's face. Then she glanced up at the sky, which seemed to grow darker by the minute. "We've lost the light," she said, holding out her hand to help Gabriella up. "Come, let us get back to the car."

"But we didn't find anything yet," Darren protested.

"It can't be helped," Ms. Therian said firmly. "Perhaps there was nothing to find. Though it is very interesting that two magic-users were patrolling the area. Very interesting, indeed."

"Why were they even here?" Gabriella asked as they began to walk back to Ms. Therian's car.

"I do not know," Ms. Therian admitted. "Perhaps they were watching to see if any Changers would come to investigate? It seems odd. There might be more to consider here than we initially thought."

"They must know something about Jai," Darren said.

"Yes," Ms. Therian agreed. "I think that is likely."

Darren clenched his fists, trying to contain the brewing lightning. "If I could've stopped them—if I could've hit them even *one* time with my lightning—we could have, I don't know, *captured* them or something!"

"Don't despair," Ms. Therian said. "Our mission may not have yielded much, but we learned something important. Auden Ironbound's servants are aware of

Jai and his mysterious disappearance. Perhaps they are even responsible. Two young magic-users, attacking right out in the open? That's very poor form. If I were their teacher, I would be livid."

In the growing darkness, Gabriella and Darren exchanged a furtive glance. Luckily, Ms. Therian didn't seem to notice.

By the time they got back into the car, Darren was glad it was dark; that way, no one could see how upset he was. During the drive back to Willow Cove, he stared out the window into the night. He knew Gabriella was right, of course. He couldn't just let his lightning continue to spiral out of control. The stakes were too high, and the results were too dangerous. A sick feeling washed over Darren as he remembered the angry red burn on the tender skin of Gabriella's ear. It looked like it hurt—a lot. And yet, she was incredibly lucky; a few inches to the left, and it would've been so much worse.

Never again, Darren thought firmly, clenching his fists once more. He had to find a way to get his Changer powers under control before he could do any more damage.

As Ms. Therian approached Darren's house, though, he realized just how hard that would be. Seeing this familiar house, the place where he'd grown up with Mom and Dad and Ray—all the happy Christmases and back-yard barbecues and patio breakfasts—felt like a knife in his heart. How had it all slipped away? Ray was gone, living at college; now Dad was leaving for good; and maybe even Darren and his mom would be moving away too. The little house just sat there, lights glowing in the windows, like everything was okay. Like it wasn't all falling apart.

Darren tried to take a deep breath, but that uncomfortable tightness was pressing down on his chest again.

"See you tomorrow, Darren," Ms. Therian said as she pulled up to the curb.

"Text me later," Gabriella added. "And have a good night."

"Thanks," Darren said, getting out of the car. "You, too."

Then he shut the door and hurried up to his house. It still felt like home, but with a big, empty space where Dad should've been. How could something that was missing feel so enormously overwhelming?

Darren's hands were hot again. Burning, even.

Get upstairs, he told himself. Alone, he could breathe; alone, he could calm down, and then he would somehow find a way to get through dinner with Mom, both of them pretending like that huge, terrible emptiness wasn't there.

"Darren! I thought I heard you come in," Mom said as she walked out of the kitchen, wiping her hands on a dish towel.

Halfway up the stairs, Darren froze. *Stay—calm—he* thought. "Hey, Mom," he said, trying to sound normal . . . and failing miserably.

Mom's welcoming smile disappeared, replaced by a look of concern. "Oh, sweetheart," she said. "Come here. Let me give you a hug."

"I'm . . . okay. I'm—just— I have a lot of homework," Darren managed to say.

Mom was quiet for a moment. "I'm not going to force you to talk about it if you're not ready," she said. "But, Darren, you can't keep your feelings locked up inside. I know how hard this is. I know how much it hurts. . . ."

Then why are you doing it to us! Darren wanted to yell. But he held his tongue, and his temper.

The lights flickered, anyway.

Mom glanced at the hall light warily. "The lights again? If this keeps up, I'm going to have to call the electrician back," she said with a sigh. "Dinner will be ready soon, Darren. I can't wait to hear about your day."

"Okay," Darren said, already making a mental list of the things he couldn't tell her: a secret mission to Fisherman's Bay, how his teacher is a werewolf, accidentally hurting his friend with a bolt of lightning from his own hands.

Darren trudged up the stairs and, finally, escaped to his bedroom. He sighed heavily as he sat down at his desk and began rummaging around in his backpack. He *really* didn't feel like doing homework right now, but maybe it would take his mind off how awful he felt. One by one, he dropped his textbooks onto the desk with a loud thud. Now he just needed his calculator and pencil case and—

What was that?

At the very bottom of his backpack, Darren's fingers brushed against something unusual. Something he didn't expect to find. He grabbed hold of it and pulled out a woven leather band that he'd never seen before. An intricate pattern of interconnected loops had been pressed into the band.

Cool, Darren thought as he slid the wristband over his hand. The leather was completely broken in, so worn and soft that it seemed to take the shape of his wrist immediately.

But where had it come from?

Ray! Darren suddenly thought. Of course. It would be just like Ray to give Darren something special, a reminder that he would always be there for him. Darren tried to think back on if he'd ever seen Ray wearing this bracelet. Maybe. It was hard to remember, since he hardly saw Ray now that his brother was in college. *I did see Ray in my room this morning before I left for school,* Darren thought. *Maybe it belongs to him. Maybe he put it in my backpack while I was brushing my teeth.* He pressed his fingers against the bracelet and smiled as he thought of his brother. The sparks brewing in his fingertips began to falter and then dimmed. Darren stared at his fingers with wondrous relief.

I can control this, he realized, *as soon as I can control my feelings, my emotions—myself.*

Ray was far away right now, and Darren could only guess what he was doing—getting pizza with his buddies, maybe, or holing up in the library for another late-night study session. But despite the physical distance between them, in that moment, Darren felt closer than ever to his big brother. Whatever Mom and Dad did, together or apart, Ray and Darren would always have each other.

Darren's phone buzzed with an e-mail. It was from Ray, which made Darren grin. It was like they were both thinking of each other at the exact same time.

Little D. Hope you're hanging in okay. I want you to know you can talk to me anytime, man. I am here for you, always. And I think Mom is going to find a counselor for you to talk to. You should do it. I dropped in at the counseling center on campus this morning and felt about a thousand times better after I talked to somebody there. Plus, a counselor is totally confidential— you can tell them anything, and they will keep it secret. Also, think about adding a couple extra workouts to your schedule. Exercise helps with stress—a lot.

Fear and anger are like poisons. Keep them inside too long, and they'll make you sick. Don't be afraid to let those emotions out. You have to trust me on this.

Love,

Ray

Darren read Ray's e-mail twice, twisting the leather band around his wrist the whole time. *If only it was that easy,* he thought sadly. He was glad that Ray had seen a counselor and found it helpful, but Darren couldn't imagine any counselor in the world who could keep all his secrets. They were too big, too overwhelming.

Darren's best friends at school, Ethan and Kyle, wouldn't come close to understanding how he felt, and as for his Changer friends . . . Well, he wasn't sure he was ready to talk to them about this sort of thing yet. Darren had really only been close to Mack, Fiona, and Gabriella for the past few months. Could he trust them to not spread it around school or to *not* look at him without some kind of pity? And he didn't want them to think he was some kind of baby who couldn't go on missions because there was stuff going on at home. . . .

No. Darren's best option—his *only* option—would be to keep what was going on at home to himself. And for the first time, with the sparks under his skin extinguished and that leather wristband pressed against his skin, Darren thought he might actually manage it.

Chapter 6
BACK IN CONTROL

Gabriella was speaking in such a low, rushed whisper that Mack had to lean in close to hear her.

"And I was trying to attack the magic-users—I'd transformed, and I just wanted to, you know, trap them or something—and Darren was supposed to back me up, and he was trying. I mean, it was totally obvious he was trying really hard, but . . ."

"But what?" Mack asked impatiently.

Gabriella shook her head. "It's like the harder he tried, the less control he had," she explained. "His lightning was flying *everywhere*. I was spending all my energy trying to dodge it. It felt—"

Gabriella's voice broke off unexpectedly.

"You can say it," Fiona said. "Whatever it is, you can tell us."

"I know it's wrong, but it almost felt like I was fighting three enemies," Gabriella finished. She looked ashamed to have spoken those words aloud.

Mack frowned. "But Darren would never try to hurt you," he said.

"Of course he wasn't *trying* to," Gabriella retorted. "But he did all the same." She flicked her long, black hair over her shoulder to reveal her left ear, which had a red, oozing welt on it.

"Darren did that?" Fiona asked incredulously. "With his lightning?"

Gabriella nodded. "I had to tell my mom I accidentally burned myself with a curling iron," she said. "It really hurts, and I don't know what I'm going to do with my hair at soccer practice today. I read that *nahuals* are supposed to have healing powers, but I haven't really developed any yet, so I can't just heal it up quickly." Gabriella paused and then sighed. "Look, I'm not telling you this to trash Darren behind his back. I'm really worried about him. I tried to tell him that he could trust me—whatever is bothering him; we're his friends, his teammates. And I know firsthand how keeping something from your teammates can mean losing—"

"Hey, guys," Darren said as he approached. "What's up?"

A heavy, uncomfortable silence fell over the group. *Oh, man. Did he hear what Gabriella was saying?* Mack worried. He racked his brain, trying to think of something, *anything* to say.

"Cool wristband," Fiona said loudly, filling the silence.

"Thanks," Darren said with an easy smile as he pressed his fingers against the leather band. He looked like he was about to say something else, but just then, Ms. Therian entered the ancillary gym, clapping her hands.

"Transformations, please. We will pick up where we left off yesterday," she announced.

Mack glanced at Darren out of the corner of his eye. Gabriella hadn't mentioned if she'd told Ms. Therian all the details of their misadventure in the woods, but he had a feeling that she probably hadn't. Mack was torn.

On the one hand, if Darren's powers really were spiraling out of control, Ms. Therian needed to know. Just thinking about the angry-looking welt on Gabriella's ear made him flinch.

But what if Ms. Therian overreacted? What if she banned Darren from missions—or even practice—before Mack and the others had a chance to reach out to Darren? To help him?

I'll just see how practice goes today, Mack finally decided as he transformed into his *kitsune* form. *If Darren really can't handle things, Ms. Therian will notice and make the decision herself.*

Even so, Mack knew he would be keeping a close eye on his friend. Darren might not think that his friends could help him, but Mack would have his back regardless.

But nobody was more surprised than Mack when Darren pulled off his best Changers class yet. In his *impundulu* form, Darren executed almost perfect flying maneuvers. He swooped through the air with utmost grace, turning on a dime and nailing every landing. And his lightning! Mack had never seen anything like it. Again and again, Darren's lightning bolts were white hot and sizzling as they sliced through the air, piercing the exact center of every one of Ms. Therian's targets.

Before long, Mack realized that he had stopped training altogether—and he wasn't the only one. Gabriella, in her *nahual* form, was standing motionless on the track, watching in wonder. In the pool, Fiona surfaced to marvel at Darren's blazing lightning, which lit up the gym like the world's most incredible fireworks display. Even Ms. Therian couldn't tear her eyes away.

Suddenly, the bell rang. Class had never run late before, and Ms. Therian looked surprised that the time had slipped away so quickly. "Finish up, everyone," she said. "Darren—that was exceptional. A truly remarkable practice. Well done."

Then Ms. Therian beckoned toward Fiona and Mack. "You two run ahead to the locker rooms. With your mission this afternoon, I'd hate for you to keep Akira waiting."

"Don't rush on my account" came a voice from the doorway. Mack turned to see that his grandfather had entered the gym so quietly, no one had noticed. *Good thing they've got so many enchantments on the doors,* Mack thought. He couldn't imagine what would happen if just anyone could stumble in.

Mack grinned and nodded to Jiichan, who smiled as he lifted his hand to return the greeting. But there was something around Jiichan's eyes that made Mack pause. Maybe it was because Mack was in his *kitsune* form, with all his senses heightened, but Mack almost felt like there was a cloud of worry hanging over his grandfather.

By the time Mack transformed a few seconds later, though, it was gone.

Or was it? Perhaps Mack, as a human, just couldn't sense it.

As Mack hurried to change back into his school clothes, he wanted to ask Jiichan what was up. He couldn't forget that brief foreboding that had emanated from his grandfather. But Mack had a feeling even if something *was* wrong, Jiichan wouldn't tell him until he was good and ready.

Darren entered the locker room then, whistling to himself.

"Dude!" Mack exclaimed. "That was incredible! I mean—*wow!*"

A grin crossed Darren's face as he ducked his head. "Well, you know, I had to make up for the other day in class," he joked. "But thanks."

"How did you do it?" Mack asked, unable to keep his curiosity under wraps.

Darren shrugged. "I wish I could tell you," he admitted. "I guess I had a breakthrough or something. I think I've learned how to control my lightning. It feels . . . It feels almost natural. Like breathing, you know?"

Mack did know. He would never forget the first time he transformed, after almost losing hope that he would ever manage it. "Well, if you figure it out, you've gotta tell the rest of us," he said. "I wish I could handle my powers so well."

"I honestly think that it starts right here," Darren said, tapping his temple. "Mind over matter."

Mack grinned wryly. "You're sounding a lot like my grandfather, so you're probably right," he cracked. "Anyway, I've got to go. Don't want to be late for the mission."

"Good luck," Darren said, serious all of a sudden. "And be careful."

"I will," Mack promised.

Back in the gym, Fiona, Ms. Therian, and Jiichan were waiting for him. "Mack, Fiona—a word before you depart," Ms. Therian said. "I'm not sure if Gabriella and Darren told you about our mission yesterday."

Mack and Fiona exchanged a glance. "Um, a little," Fiona said carefully.

"Then you probably know that they were besieged by a witch and warlock at Fisherman's Bay," Ms. Therian said. "I don't want to scare you before your mission, but I do want you to be on highest alert."

"We will be," Fiona replied.

"This is a promising sign, I think," Ms. Therian continued. "They are worried about us, or else they would not be on patrol. And they are sloppy—that much is certain. This ought to give us a chance to resolve Jai's disappearance before they strike again."

"Strike again?" Mack repeated. "You—you think that's a possibility?"

This time, it was Ms. Therian and Jiichan's turn to exchange a glance.

"It is not a possibility, Makoto," Jiichan finally replied, "but a certainty."

"Unless we can stop them first," added Ms. Therian. "Go. And good luck. I look forward to your report."

Half an hour later, Jiichan pulled his car into the driveway of a modest, one-story house on a quiet street in Middletown. "Here we are," he said.

Jai's father must have been watching for them because he opened the front door before they were even halfway up the path. "Akira. Thank you for coming," he said. "Please come in."

Once they were inside, Jiichan placed one hand on Fiona's shoulder and the other on Mack's shoulder. "Ankur, thank you for your warm welcome," he said. "May I present my grandson, Makoto, a *kitsune*, and Fiona Murphy, a *selkie*."

Ankur nodded to each of them. "It is an honor to meet you," he said. "I know my son would have—"

Ankur's voice caught in this throat, and his piercing brown eyes grew watery. "I apologize," he said, pressing his hands over his eyes. "I'm terribly worried for him."

"We will not stop searching until he is found and returned to you," Jiichan assured him. "May we sit?"

"Yes, yes, of course," Ankur replied, gesturing toward the living room. "I've made tea. Please, make yourselves comfortable."

Mack accepted an earthenware mug filled with fragrant chai. He took a sip of the sweet tea, tasting cloves, ginger, cinnamon, and other spices he couldn't quite place. It was delicious.

"Why don't you tell us about how Jai came into his powers," Jiichan suggested to Ankur.

Ankur grimaced. "I should've noticed," he said. Then he turned to Mack and Fiona. "We are *naga*," he explained. "Serpent Changers. We hold sway over water: directing its course, summoning it in floods, withholding it in droughts. In ancient times we were the guardians of lakes, rivers, and streams.

"I had a strong feeling that Jai was also a *naga*, but I came into my powers later than most," Ankur explained. "I was nearly fifteen before they awakened. Never in my wildest dreams did I expect Jai's powers to show themselves so soon. He's just eleven."

"That took us *all* by surprise," Jiichan said.

"After what happened . . ."

"The flood in Middletown?" Fiona said.

Ankur nodded. "He didn't know what was happening. He didn't know how to control the raw power. He was scared—so scared—and he told no one what was happening. His fear grew and grew, until it manifested into the terrible flood. It was my fault. If I'd been paying attention, if I'd seen the signs . . ."

Mack thought back to the news coverage he'd seen about the Middletown flood. A dozen families had lost their homes.

"Jai must have been devastated," Fiona said. "How did he react?"

"Jai is a good boy," Ankur said. "He has a good heart. After the flood . . . He blamed himself, and there was not a thing I could say or do that would ease his guilt. It consumed him; I watched my boy draw within himself. I tried to begin his Changer training, but he was uninterested. He thought if he ignored his powers, they would go away. And strangely enough—"

"His powers disappeared?" Mack interrupted.

"Not at all," Ankur said. "But he was suddenly able to exert complete control over them."

"Did this arouse your suspicions?" asked Jiichan.

"Perhaps it should've," Ankur admitted. "But I already knew that Jai was an unusual Changer. I thought that rapid advancements in his powers might be something to expect. And he seemed happy again. Calm. Like he had everything figured out. It was . . . It was a welcome change, after all we'd been through. I didn't want to question it."

"What happened next?" asked Fiona.

Ankur ran a hand through his hair anxiously, gluing his eyes to the floor. "He didn't come home," he replied.

"Do you have a photo of Jai?" Fiona asked. "Something recent, like from right before he disappeared?"

"I do," Ankur replied as he reached into his shirt pocket for his phone. "I took these the night before he vanished. See? You see how happy he looks? Content."

Fiona took the phone and studied the screen. Suddenly, all the color drained from her face, as if she'd seen a ghost . . .

Or something even worse.

Chapter 7
GONE

Fiona didn't want to alarm anyone. She wasn't the type to jump to conclusions—not about something as serious as this. But her hands were trembling, ever so slightly, and her heart was pounding. Because what she'd seen in that photo—something small, something most people never would've noticed—had filled her with a terrible sense of foreboding. Fiona had never met Jai; she had never even seen his picture before, but there was something in the photo that was immediately recognizable to her: Jai was wearing the same imprinted leather wristband that Darren had on in Changers class.

And Darren did so great today, Fiona thought, her mind

whirling. *Just like Ankur said that Jai's powers were suddenly under control.*

It couldn't be a coincidence.

Or could it?

A small part of Fiona was tempted to tell everybody her theory, right then and there. Why not let Mr. Kimura figure out what to do next? But if she was wrong—if she caused a whole lot of trouble over a whole lot of nothing—or worse, if she got Ankur's hopes up for no reason . . .

Fiona shook her head, just a little. *I've got to be certain,* she thought. *One hundred percent, no-doubt-about-it certain.*

"Ankur, could I have copies of these photos?" she asked, scrolling through the others and hoping she sounded normal. She glanced from face to face. If anyone in the room had noticed her unease, they weren't showing it.

"Yes, of course," he said. "You can go ahead and send them to yourself, if you want."

Fiona tapped at the screen until she had texted herself three different photos of Jai. In each one, the leather wristband was clearly displayed. As soon as she could see Darren's wristband in comparison to the one Jai was wearing in the photos, she would know for sure.

And then, Fiona hoped, she would know what to do next.

Somehow, Fiona managed to avoid spilling all the details of her theory during the drive back to Willow Cove. But by the time they approached her house, she was about to burst with the secret.

"Mack," she said. "Do you want to study together for our math test?"

"Our math test?" Mack repeated, looking confused.

Fiona tried not to groan in frustration. "Yes," she said, very clearly. "Our math test tomorrow. We can study together now. You could even stay for dinner, I'm sure. If you want."

Mack still looked clueless, so Fiona gave his ankle a swift kick.

"Oh!" he said suddenly. "Right! That math test. I forgot. Jiichan, do you mind if I go over to Fiona's house to study?"

From the front seat, Mr. Kimura chuckled. "If you forgot you even had an exam, I think studying with Fiona is an excellent idea," he said. "Call me when you are finished, and I'll come to pick you up."

"Thanks, Jiichan," Mack said as he and Fiona climbed out of the car. As his grandfather drove away, Mack turned to Fiona. "This better be good," he said, leaning over to rub his ankle, "because that hurt!"

"Sorry," Fiona murmured. "I didn't know how else to get your attention. Listen, I think I found a big clue."

Mack looked intrigued. "Since we met with Ankur?" he asked.

"Actually, during," Fiona corrected him. She held up her phone so he could see one of the photos of Jai.

Mack stared at the screen for several seconds. "Okay, what am I missing?" he finally asked.

"The wristband," Fiona replied at once. "Check it out! I think it's identical to the one Darren was wearing in class today!"

A skeptical frown crossed Mack's face. "Are you sure?" he asked, zooming in on the photo. "It's similar . . . I think. To be honest, I didn't get a really good look at Darren's wristband. It was leather, right?"

"Yes," Fiona said. "With the same pattern imprinted on it."

Mack continued to examine the photo. "Maybe," he said slowly. Then he gave Fiona her phone. "But I'm not totally convinced. Leather accessories are really popular. A lot of people wear them. Even me."

Mack reached under the collar of his shirt to pull out his fox-tooth necklace, a gift from his grandfather that hung on a sturdy leather cord around his neck.

"They probably even got their wristbands from the same store," Mack continued. "It's not like those things are custom-made."

Fiona shook her head. "I don't think so," she said. "And the stories match up. Ankur said that Jai got his powers mysteriously under control right before he disappeared. And look at how Darren aced practice today—he was incredible! Like a complete and total reversal from yesterday and the day before!"

"Yeah," Mack admitted. "That was . . . unexpected."

"I don't know how to explain it, but I think there's a pattern here," Fiona said as she started to pace back and forth in the driveway. "Like . . . imagine this: A group of warlocks who are targeting Changer kids having trouble controlling their powers. Somehow, they slip them a leather wristband that . . . that . . ."

"What?" Mack asked.

"I'm not sure," Fiona said. "Maybe it gives them a false sense of confidence. Maybe it controls their abilities for them. Maybe it's a tracking device. The thing is, I wouldn't be a bit surprised if the other kids who disappeared were also wearing a leather wristband right before they vanished."

"Why don't we tell Jiichan and Ms. Therian your theory?" Mack suggested. "Maybe they'll be able to fill in the blanks for us."

"Yeah, I guess we should do that," Fiona said. "But we have to reach Darren first. At the very least he needs to take that wristband *off* before something happens to him!"

With flying fingers, Fiona called Darren and then put her phone on speaker. One ring, two rings, three— and then, to her relief, Darren's voice crackled over her phone.

"Hey, Fiona, what's up?"

"Darren," she began, skipping all pleasantries. "That leather wristband you were wearing today—where did you get it?"

"My wristband?" Darren said. "My brother gave it to me."

Mack caught Fiona's eye and mouthed, *Told you so*, but a nagging, insistent feeling made her press on.

"I know this might sound weird, but would you mind if Mack and I came over to take a look at it?" she asked.

"You want to see my wristband?" Darren asked, sounding confused. "Yeah, that's fine, I guess. But I'm not home right now. Football practice."

"Oh, right," replied Fiona. "Well, how about after?"

"Sure, if it's so important to you," Darren said. "I'll text you when I get home, and you can come over."

"When will that be?" Fiona asked.

"Like, fifteen minutes," Darren said. "Listen, I have to go before Coach catches me on the phone and makes me run drills for the rest of the week. I'll text you soon."

And with that, he hung up.

Fiona and Mack exchanged a long look.

"He thinks I'm crazy," she said.

"I wouldn't worry about it," Mack told her. "Better safe than sorry, right? We'll head over to Darren's in a little bit, check out the wristband. When we see it in person, it will probably be completely different from the one Jai had."

"I hope so," Fiona said, but she didn't sound convinced. And she couldn't seem to stop pacing, even after she and Mack went inside to start their homework. Her phone was sitting right there on the table, but the text she was waiting for never arrived.

"It's been a half hour!" she exclaimed impatiently. "Why hasn't he texted?"

Mack shrugged. "Maybe practice ran long," he replied. "Maybe he's still changing out of his gear. Maybe he forgot."

Fiona shook her head. "I have a bad feeling," she said. "I'm going to text him." She typed as fast as she could:

> Darren—All done?

Then they waited. And waited. An agonizing ten minutes passed before Fiona finally grabbed her coat.

"What are you doing?" asked Mack.

"I'm going over to Darren's house," she replied. "Either he'll be there, or we'll be waiting for him when he finally gets home. I can't just sit around here worrying like this."

"Okay," Mack replied. "Let's go."

Fiona told her father that she and Mack were going for a quick ride and then grabbed her bike from the shed. Mack borrowed her father's bike. Then they rode through Willow Cove as the sun began to set and one by one, the streetlights flickered on. The unsteady buzz as they first illuminated reminded Fiona of the trouble Darren experienced with his powers—until he'd suddenly shown up with that unusual wristband.

She pedaled faster.

As Fiona and Mack turned the corner on to Darren's street, they saw even more lights. But these lights were not the steady, golden glow of the streetlights; they were red and blue, flashing in a rapid pattern. They were warning lights.

Police lights.

"Oh no," Fiona said breathlessly as she saw the police car parked in Darren's driveway. "No, no, no."

"Come on," Mack urged her, a frightened look in his eyes.

They dropped the bikes onto the sidewalk and ran up the driveway, past the patrol car where one of the officers was on the radio. "Yeah, probably a runaway. Problems at home. You know the type," he was saying.

"A *runaway*"? "*Problems at home*"? Fiona wondered. There was no way the officer could be talking about Darren—he didn't even *know* him. But before she could interrupt, another officer approached them.

"Hey, kids," she began.

Just then, Darren's mom ran out of the house. "Fiona! Mack!" she cried. "Have you seen Darren? Is he with you?"

"No, he isn't," Fiona replied. "He— We were supposed to meet him here. Like an hour ago. You mean he's not here?"

Mrs. Smith's whole face crumpled up as she shook her head. "No," she said, choking on a sob. "He never made it home."

Chapter 8
THE MISSING CHANGERS

Darren wasn't sure where he was. He wasn't even sure whether or not he was awake. It was like a third state, somewhere in-between, where everything was filtered through a hazy glow: sound and sight; touch, even. A sludgy weakness oozed through his body, making him feel heavy and dull. Darren was aware of all this, but the funny thing was that he didn't really care. Everything was fine. It was all fine. Maybe he should sleep a little longer. That would be fine too.

But something inside him—some small, ferocious spark—didn't want to do that.

Open your eyes, it hissed. *Open your eyes.*

Darren didn't see the point. Besides, his eyelids felt as scratchy as sandpaper. That small, insistent voice wouldn't quit, however; not until he forced his eyes open, blinked a few times, and waited for everything to come into focus. He was in a strange room, a library of sorts, with built-in bookshelves that held thousands of books. The books weren't the strange part, though. No, it was the tall pedestal in the center of the room—marble streaked with steely gray veins—that made Darren feel cold all over, despite the roaring fire in the fireplace.

Now, move your arms, the voice inside told him. *Move your legs.*

Darren tried. Failed.

What . . . , he wondered as the power of thought slowly returned to him. He looked down, and that's when he realized that he was tied up. Heavy ropes as thick as his wrist had him bound to a wooden chair.

No way, Darren thought as that spark inside him flared, bolder and brighter this time. He strained against the ropes, but they wouldn't budge. That wasn't a problem, though. He would just transform, or blast his way out with a blazing bolt of lightning.

But nothing happened.

Darren tried—again and again and again—but it was almost as if his powers were gone. Completely, totally, and utterly gone.

A thin film of sweat formed across Darren's forehead as he glanced around the room. That's when he noticed at least three other chairs arranged in a circle around the pedestal. Each chair had a motionless kid tied to it. Perhaps most disturbing, the kids were all breathing with the same slow, steady motion: *in* and *out*, *in* and *out*, as if even that was being controlled for them.

"Pssst."

The whisper was so faint that at first Darren wondered if he had imagined it. He turned his head to the left and noticed that another boy next to him was awake—and he was staring at Darren.

"Hey!" Darren said. "What— Who—"

"Don't struggle. It'll just make things worse."

"Where are we? Who are you?"

"I don't know—I woke up here too. I'm Jai," the boy said.

Jai.

Darren sucked in his breath sharply. He'd found Jai! He had no idea how he'd done it. Actually, he had no idea how a lot of things had come to pass. But here was Jai, the missing boy whom they'd been searching for.

Darren's entire body went rigid with tension.

Jai. The missing boy.

If Darren was with *him*, did that mean that he was missing too?

Darren's mouth was very dry, but he finally managed to ask, "What's going on?"

"I'm not sure," Jai whispered back. "But I think it's for a spell."

"A spell?" Darren repeated, trying to understand. If only his brain didn't feel so foggy and cluttered.

"We're all Changers," Jai whispered back. "I mean, you are one, right?"

"Yeah," replied Darren.

"I think they needed to gather all the elements," Jai said. "That much I could figure out. See, I'm water, and that girl on my other side is a phoenix, so she has fire. The other girl—she's been knocked out for a while—but the phoenix said she's a *púca*, so earth. And that guy across from you?

He's a *tengu*, a bird with power over wind. What are you?"

"Lightning," Darren said, feeling a little sick.

Jai nodded knowingly. "Of course. Energy to bring the elements together."

"But what do they want from us?" Darren asked.

"I don't know," Jai replied. "Every time I start asking questions, they knock me out again."

"Is that what happened to them?" Darren said, nodding toward the other kids, who were all still breathing in perfect, unsettling unison.

Jai shook his head. "No. It was worse. They tried to escape."

Suddenly, Jai's shoulders stiffened, and even in the dimly lit room, Darren could see the fear flash through his eyes. "They're coming," he murmured. "Be careful!"

Darren sat very still. Then he heard it too: steady, even footsteps, growing louder. Coming closer.

Five witches and warlocks entered the room then; each one positioned him- or herself behind a chair. Darren tried to twist around to see who was standing behind him, but a swift, hard kick to his chair jolted his head so he was facing forward.

"Don't move," a deep voice growled. "And keep your mouth shut."

A heavy silence filled the room, thick with anticipation and fear.

The double doors to the library creaked loudly on their hinges, and a tall man who was impossibly thin glided into the room. In his arms he carried a bundle, something draped in gold velvet that cast an otherworldly gleam on his face. It wasn't quite a smile that crossed his lips, but something far more sinister—a look of triumph.

The warlock behind Darren's chair moved to meet the strange man.

"We've found the last youngling, as instructed, Jasper," said the warlock.

"Then we must make haste. The First Four will be hunting for him even as we speak."

With great care, as though carrying a newborn baby, Jasper brought the bundle across the room and placed it atop the pedestal. Then he pulled a piece of black chalk from his pocket and began to draw a series of symbols on the floor around the pedestal. The symbols looked familiar to Darren, and it took a moment, but he soon realized that they had formed a pattern of interlocking circles that was remarkably similar to the design on his wristband.

I *have to get out of here*, Darren thought, panic rising in his chest. He struggled against the ropes, but the warlock behind him grabbed his shoulders and held tight.

When Jasper finished the markings, he stepped up to the pedestal and removed the velvet cloth to reveal the Horn of Power. Darren recognized it at once. The sight of it filled him with dread, even though he could still see the long, ugly crack Mack had made in it during their first battle with Auden Ironbound. Jasper's long, thin fingers traced the crack, making it glow with cold light.

They're trying to fix it, Darren thought suddenly. He *had* to escape—but how?

Just then, Jasper began muttering words in a language that Darren had never heard before. Darren's wristband began to glow, emitting a beam of golden light. He glanced wildly around the room, only to have his worst suspicions confirmed: Each Changer had the same wristband, and each wristband had begun to glow.

It wasn't from Ray at all, Darren realized. He'd never felt so stupid in his entire life. There he was, desperate for a sign that his family would be okay—that everything would be okay—that he had convinced himself that Ray had reached out to him. But why would Ray have left the wristband in secret? No note? No text? Now that Darren took the time to consider it, it didn't make sense.

Wanting and wishing doesn't make something real, Darren thought bitterly, longing to rip the cursed band off his wrist and throw it into the fireplace, where the flames had begun to burn a supernatural green. It had been a trap all along, and Darren had fallen right into it.

I've let everyone down, he thought miserably. Ms. Therian and Mr. Kimura and Sefu and Yara and Mack and Gabriella and Fiona. Fiona. She tried to warn me, she was worried, but I didn't listen.

Darren's breath caught in his throat, ragged and uneven. And now they'll be at risk, he thought. The horn will be repaired, and all the Changers in the world will be under Auden Ironbound's command.

Darren's wrist was hurting. Hurting bad. The wristband was vibrating, and Darren could feel his bones trembling along with it. Suddenly, a tremulous bolt of lightning burst from the wristband. It crackled across the room until it made contact with the pedestal. It was a puny bolt, but as the pain in Darren's bones increased, so did the bolt's strength. By his side, he could see the wristband forcing Jai to conjure water as well, and across from him, a torrent of wind was emanating from the *tengu*. That's when Darren realized that the wristband was pulling all their powers from them—and using them for the worst evil of all.

The spark in Darren roared into a blazing fire. It burned away his fear, his sadness, his shame, and his regret, leaving only one emotion intact: a deep and pure sense of purpose. His lightning was his own; it belonged to *him*, and there was no way he was going to let Auden Ironbound's henchmen use it to hurt his friends.

But not even Darren could've predicted what happened next.

Sparks of energy exploded from the wristband, tearing it in two and sending a massive bolt of lightning—Darren's lightning, made by him, *controlled by him*—straight into the air. It destroyed the ropes that bound him, blasted the ceiling off the library, and shot straight into the sky. On the floor, the marble pedestal cracked in half.

Through the gaping hole above, Darren saw the stars. They looked so close, and brighter than ever—

Then everything went dark.

Chapter 9
Battle at Elmbridge

The tea had grown cold; food sat on the table, untouched. The First Four were in the kitchen at Mack's house, talking in low voices as they tried to figure out a plan. It was getting late, but Fiona was only vaguely aware of the time. Sitting on the living room floor with *The Compendium* on her lap, she focused all her attention on searching for information about Darren's mysterious disappearance. Fiona didn't know what she was looking for, exactly, but *The Compendium* had the answers to just about everything— even to questions that had not yet been asked.

"I can't even read this," Mack complained from across the room as he stared at a stack of yellowed parchment pages. "I mean, what is this, invisible ink? I can barely see anything here."

"It might be," Fiona said thoughtfully. "I saw something about a potion for ink that could only be read by the Changer who created it."

"Well, that seems pretty pointless," Mack replied.

"Hang on," Fiona said abruptly.

"Did you find something?" asked Gabriella.

Fiona frowned in concentration as she scanned the page. "Maybe," she said. "Listen to this. 'The Circlet of Subjugation. It is not their appearance that impresses so much as what these binding ties can accomplish: the wholesale harnessing of another Changer's powers, whether or not he or she wills it. Indeed, their unassuming appearance has played an important role in the defeat of many unsuspecting Changers. Though rare, some Changers have been able to overcome and break the Circlet through an intense burst of power.'"

"The wristband?" Mack guessed.

"It's possible," Fiona replied. "I wish there was a description of them—or a drawing, or even info about how they're formed."

"Dark magic, I bet," Gabriella said, wrapping her arms around herself.

"Jiichan and the others might know more about them," Mack suggested. He stood up and started walking toward the kitchen.

But he never made it.

At that moment the entire house began to shake.

An *earthquake,* Fiona thought, pressing *The Compendium* to her chest as if to protect it. But even as those words formed in her mind, she knew how wrong they were. This was no earthquake. There was something far more powerful behind it. Fiona squeezed her eyes shut tight, as if to see with another sense. Suddenly, she, Mack, and Gabriella cried out in unison: "Darren!"

The First Four were by their side in an instant.

"What did you see?" Ms. Therian asked urgently.

Fiona shook her head. "I— It's more like I can *feel* him," she said haltingly.

"He's close," Mack added.

"But he's in trouble. He's trying to fight something off," Gabriella finished.

"Let's go," Mr. Kimura said.

"Are we going to drive?" Gabriella asked, looking perplexed by the sudden turn of events.

"No time," Yara said, sounding more sprightly than ever. "Backyard?" she asked, turning to Mr. Kimura.

"Yes. That would be best," he replied.

Everyone followed Mr. Kimura to his perfectly manicured rock garden, where the gnarled bonsai cast strange shadows in the light of the moon. The world began to shake again, and this time Fiona could see why: in the distance, a bizarre bolt of lightning struck in reverse, blasting from the earth to the clouds instead of the other way around.

"Elmbridge?" Sefu asked in a low voice.

"Yes," Ms. Therian replied. "There's no doubt in my mind."

"Come closer," Mr. Kimura said. When everyone was standing in a tight circle, Mr. Kimura made a strange motion with his hands. Fiona watched in amazement as she seemed to fade away, leaving only the faintest outline of herself behind.

"A cloaking illusion," Ms. Therian explained, anticipating Fiona's question. "As close to invisibility as we can manage with a group this size, and easily reversed when the time is right." The five land Changers transformed; then Ms. Therian and Mr. Kimura knelt down so that Fiona and Yara could climb onto their backs. Fiona had never ridden on a werewolf before; she grabbed fistfuls of Ms. Therian's coarse fur and held on for dear life as the werewolf began to gallop toward the lightning.

The world passed by in a blur as the Changers moved at top speed. Fiona could feel the thundering of their paws more than she could hear them. All the while they raced toward the strange lightning, a better beacon to lead them to Darren than Fiona ever dreamed they would have.

It seemed like just seconds passed before they arrived at a decrepit mansion deep in the woods. A weathered sign read faintly: ELMBRIDGE ESTATE. The darkness would have been all-consuming, but Darren's lightning bolt shone as brightly as the sun—and a good thing, too, since Fiona suddenly shrieked, "Look out!"

There was an army of witches and warlocks approaching them, their curses crackling through the night air. Ms. Therian tried to shield her, for which

Fiona was grateful. Outside of the water, her *selkie* transformation was useless, and her magic was still bound up in the *selkie* songs, which she could only learn from another *selkie*. Fiona watched as Gabriella and Mack took on a warlock by themselves, helping to clear the way up the mansion steps. *When will it be my turn to fight like that?* Fiona thought. *When will I get to use my magic to protect my friends?*

Luckily, the First Four were able to handle the warlocks and witches with ease. All Fiona had to do was stay out of the way. She had never seen the First Four using their powers together. Their skills and strategies were utterly captivating, but as much as she wanted to watch the battle, it was hard to draw her eyes away from the stunning lightning bolt.

At last it was quiet outside. Fiona held her breath, waiting for the next wave of warlocks and witches to attack.

But they never came.

Proceed with caution, Mr. Kimura's voice rang in her head—and in everyone else's too, she suspected. As quickly as they dared, they approached the mansion.

Fiona stared up at it with apprehension. The building was enormous. Who knew how many witches and warlocks were inside? Was this just a trap, set to lure them in and destroy them?

There was only one way to find out.

Just moments after they crossed the threshold, two warlocks appeared, curses glimmering at their fingertips. Fiona felt a rush of air as Mack and Gabriella, both still in their Changer forms, passed her and tackled them. Once again, she felt that pinch of longing. It was almost unbearable to be so useless; so completely and totally useless.

I'm deadweight, Fiona thought. *Why do they even bring me on land missions?*

Then she shook her head and pushed forward through the dank hall. *It's not about me,* she reminded herself. *It's about Darren—and Jai and all the others who disappeared—and rescuing them, no matter what it takes.*

The same feeling that had alerted Fiona and the other kids to Darren's location back at Mack's house came to her again. She paused for just a moment to turn her focus inward. Something was telling her to climb the sweeping staircase up, up, up to the third floor of the mansion.

She moved forward—as if in a dream, as if there was only one path that she was ever destined to take, as if every step in her life had led her to precisely this moment.

Fiona glanced at the others, wondering if they felt it too.

That's when she noticed everyone's fur was standing up on end. Not from fear, though. From an electrical charge. Even Fiona's ordinary human hair was floating in the air, as if the force of gravity had abandoned her.

She took the stairs two at a time. There was a doorway at the far end of the corridor, and a blinding light spilled from it.

Darren's in there! Mack thought to them as he charged forward—or tried to charge forward. Before he could go more than a few steps, Mr. Kimura nipped at his neck.

Caution, Makoto, Mr. Kimura ordered. *We approach as one.*

Together, they crept forward in a tight group. Fiona knew it was no coincidence that she and Yara, still in their human forms, were huddled in the center, sur-rounded by everyone else for protection.

As they approached the blazing room, Fiona heard a strange creaking, one that filled her with fear. It was the doors; heavy wooden doors that were now splintered and destroyed, swinging from their hinges even though there was no breeze. There was another force moving through the air instead—electricity—invisible, imper-ceptible, and more dangerous than Fiona could begin to imagine. She mustered all her courage and stepped past the broken doors, shielding her eyes from the glare.

Nothing in the room was as it should be; Fiona could tell right away. A crackling, buzzing spider web of elec-trical current flickered throughout the room, holding everything within it—books, papers, even people—aloft. Everyone and everything floated on the current, motionless.

Then Fiona saw something that made her heart lurch. "Darren!"

They had found him. Darren was in the center of the room, his blank eyes glowing with white light, and he was emanating electricity from every inch of his body.

Chapter 10
SPIRIT-WALKING

A quick flash, and Gabriella transformed into her human self. "Darren!" she screamed. She tried to run toward him, but the First Four wouldn't let her. In an instant they had transformed back too.

"Let me go!" Gabriella cried as she struggled against Mr. Kimura's grasp.

"Gabriella, he's not there," Mr. Kimura said in a terribly quiet voice.

Gabriella forced herself to take a deep breath. "What do you mean?" she asked, her voice trembling. "Of course he is!"

"We have seen this happen before, when a Changer

is under extreme stress," Mr. Kimura explained. He kept his hands on her shoulders, though the tightness of his grip loosened when he realized that Gabriella wasn't going to charge forward.

"Darren used all his power in defense against . . . whatever was happening in here," Ms. Therian said as her eyes glanced at the cracked pedestal. "He is in a . . ." Her voice trailed off as she glanced to Yara for assistance.

"It's more than sleep," Yara said. "It's like a trance, almost. In a last-ditch effort, Changers of remarkable power can unleash their ability blindly to save themselves—but their senses are muted to the real world. At this moment Darren is only aware of the world within his own mind."

Sefu shook his head in dismay. "Never, *never* have I seen this happen in one so young," he said softly.

Something in his voice kindled Gabriella's fear— and her fight. She flexed her fingers and felt the razor-sharp edges of her *nahual* claws brush against the soft skin of her palms. "But there's something we can *do*, right?" she asked. "There has to be something we can do!"

Mr. Kimura looked at her. "There is something *you* can do," he replied.

"Anything," Gabriella said at once.

"No, Akira," Sefu said, speaking right over Gabriella. "She isn't ready. We should summon Rosa—"

Mr. Kimura raised his hand, signaling for calm. "Rosa would never make it in time. Gabriella is his only chance."

"Whatever it is, I want to help," Gabriella insisted.

"Listen to me first, and then make your decision," Mr. Kimura told her. "To save Darren you must spirit-walk, Gabriella—slip into Darren's own unconsciousness— and find a way to bring him back with you to this world. It's an advanced *nahual* technique, one that takes decades to master. Your aunt has only just recently come into this power."

The only sound in the shattered room—it must have been a library since there were bookshelves everywhere—was the faint buzzing from the electrical currents. Gabriella weighed Mr. Kimura's words. Spirit-walking? She'd heard of it before but never really imagined doing it herself. *I guess there's a first time for everything,* Gabriella thought.

"Gabriella, wait," Ms. Therian said just as Gabriella

was about to answer. "You barely know what Akira is asking of you—or the risks. Spirit-walking is highly dangerous, even for advanced adult *nahuals*. When you leave your body, you run the risk of forgetting how to return to it—or even forgetting why you'd want to. Then your spirit has no choice but to roam the wide world, forever searching for something that it can no longer find."

Gabriella swallowed hard, staring uncertainly at Ms. Therian. "But . . . can't you just wake me up?" she asked. "There must be some spell, or something from *The Compendium*—"

Ms. Therian shook her head. "It is not so easy, I'm afraid," she said. "There is no such thing as a spirit alarm clock. What is done will be done by you alone, on your own terms. If you spirit-walk, we *cannot* help you, even if the worst comes to pass."

"I don't like this," Sefu said. "She is but a child, she cannot fully understand . . ."

A strange calmness overcame Gabriella then; her fists relaxed, and her claws retracted. "But I do understand," she said. "I'm willing to take the risk. Any risk, if that's what it takes to save Darren. I have to *try*, at least—he would do the same for me. I know it."

No one spoke, but Gabriella thought she saw a glimmer of respect in Mr. Kimura's eyes. She turned to face him again. "So . . . spirit-walking. How do I do it?"

"I'll use my powers to hypnotize you into a deep sleep," Yara told her. "You will awaken in a dream. Now, this is very important, Gabriella: you must *remember* that it is a dream. That kind of awareness in a dream-state is what will give you the power to reach Darren."

"I understand," Gabriella said again. "So, when I realize I'm dreaming—"

"You must will yourself out of your own dream and into Darren's," Yara said. "It's hard to explain, but I think you'll understand what to do when it's happening to you. When you find him, Gabriella—listen carefully, this is also important—you must convince him to wake up immediately, for your sake as well as his. If he doesn't wake up, the chance of you finding your body again is very slim."

Yara paused to gesture toward Darren, whose skin had a sickly gray cast that was highlighted by his vacant white eyes. "He can't keep this up forever," Yara continued. "If you don't reach him in time, he will exhaust his powers. And if *that* happens, we will lose him."

A terrible silence fell over the group. As Gabriella looked at the old woman's face, she understood the stakes all too well.

Gabriella took a deep breath. "Okay," she said, marveling at how normal she sounded; there wasn't a trace of fear in her voice, though her heart was pounding. "Let's do this."

"Go ahead and lie down," Yara said.

Gabriella lay on the floor and stared up into the faces gathered around her, where she saw so much love and encouragement. "You can do it," Fiona whispered, reaching down to squeeze Gabriella's hand.

"See you when you wake up," added Mack.

Then everyone took a step back, except for Yara. She ran her hands through the air above Gabriella's body, and even though Yara never touched her, Gabriella felt the sensation of an impossibly heavy blanket covering her.

Wait, she thought, fighting against her eyes, which were trying to close. *There was something I wanted to ask. . . .*

But it was too late. Her eyes closed, anyway.

When she awoke, Gabriella was deeply dreaming. It was a glorious day at the New Brighton Zoo. She grinned as she watched her little sister, Maritza, skip ahead in the sunlight. With Ma on one side and Tía Rosa on the other, Gabriella had never been happier.

Then it was just her and Ma. Where were Maritza and Tía Rosa?

Had they been there at all?

"Beautiful creatures," Ma said, nodding toward the jaguar enclosure.

"Beautiful," Gabriella echoed. She stared at the jaguars, sleeping in the sun, and longed to join them.

Her mind was so *fuzzy*.

"Here, *mija*," Ma was saying. "Have some popcorn before I eat the whole thing."

"Thanks," Gabriella tried to say, but she couldn't quite remember how to say the word. She reached out her hand—

"Monster!" Ma screamed, staring at her in horror and backing away.

Gabriella looked down and saw velvety black fur creeping down toward her fingers. *This isn't how I transform*, she thought with confusion as one by one, her claws popped out of her fingertips. *Not in slow-motion; not like this* . . .

And then it hit her. She didn't transform like this because *this* wasn't real. *It's just a dream*, Gabriella told herself, and a sense of control surged through her.

She closed her golden cat's eyes. *I am leaving this dream*, she thought, not sure where the words were coming from, but knowing, somehow, that they were the right ones. *I am leaving this dream for Darren's dream.*

She began to walk, and with every step, the zoo melted away into a silvery mist. In an instant she was surrounded by energy, the energy that flowed through every living being—and there had never been anything else, ever.

Darren's dream, Gabriella repeated, trying not to lose focus. *Darren's dream.*

The mist swirled—began to take shape, and through it she could see the solid physicality return to everything around her—until Gabriella was back in the hall outside the library. There was Fiona and Mack and Ms. Therian and Mr. Kimura and Sefu and tiny Yara, bent over—

Gabriella swallowed hard as she stared down at her human self, still and unmoving. Her face was frozen like a mask. *It's like I'm not even there*, she realized.

Because she wasn't.

Gabriella turned away from the eerie sight and looked at Darren. His body seemed stretched to its limits, contorted by the beams of electricity that spangled the room. His head was wobbling in a strange and unsteady way.

Then Gabriella noticed for the first time that the Horn of Power was at his feet.

The tremendous crack that had nearly split the horn in two was almost gone, as if it had been expertly mended. Now it was no wider than a single hairbreadth, and it glowed with golden healing light.

So that's what this is all about, Gabriella thought as everything began to make sense.

She padded across the room toward Darren, dodging the beams of electricity, and placed her wide, velvety paws on his shoulders. There was a pulling sensation—a rushing sound, a vortex of swirling winds . . .

And just like that, Gabriella disappeared.

Chapter II
NOT ALONE

After Darren blacked out he spent a long time in a fuzzy haze, trying to get a grasp on what was going on around him. Slowly the world came into focus, but it wasn't the scene he was expecting.

"Merry Christmas!"

Darren had just opened his eyes when—*thwoomp*—Ray whacked him in the head with a pillow and started laughing hysterically.

"Aw, come on," Darren groaned, but he'd barely gotten the words out before Ray thwoomped him again.

"Get up, lazybones!" Ray bellowed. "It's Christmas!"

Darren sat up in bed and looked around him. Hadn't

he just been doing something? It had seemed so important a minute ago, but now ...

Ray's pillow came sailing through the air again, but this time, Darren was ready. He expertly blocked it and then hit Ray with his own pillow.

"Last one downstairs has to eat *all* of Grandma's fruitcake!" Darren shouted, dodging around Ray to get a head start. He reached the stairs first, but Ray was right behind him, yanking on the sash of Darren's bathrobe, until they were thundering down the steps side by side, sounding like a herd of wild elephants.

"Hey, guys, careful on the stairs!" Mom called out, but Darren could see from the grin on her face that she was as excited as he and Ray were.

Then Darren saw the Christmas tree, and it stopped him in his tracks. "Whoa," he said breathlessly.

"Whoa," Ray repeated.

The presents ... It was like a tidal wave of gifts, spilling out from under the tree until they reached halfway across the living room floor. Darren and Ray dove in immediately in a flurry of flying ribbons and ripped wrapping paper.

"What? You're not going to wait for your old man?" Dad joked as he entered from the kitchen. The tray in his hands was laden with four steaming mugs of hot chocolate, each topped with a swirl of whipped cream and a dusting of cinnamon. There was a platter of gingerbread cookies, too—all the little gingerbread people that Darren and Ray had decorated the night before, until a frosting-and-candy fight had erupted that was even more fun than cookie decorating.

Darren grinned at Dad as he abandoned the pile of presents. "Merry Christmas, Dad," he said as he bounded over to his father. Eating cookies for breakfast on Christmas morning was one of Darren's favorite family traditions.

"Merry Christmas, son," Dad replied as he leaned over to kiss the top of Darren's head. "You know I'm just kidding around. You go ahead and get back to those gifts!"

But Darren hesitated. There was something in his bathrobe pocket, something he'd carefully wrapped and placed there last night, all in anticipation of this moment. Darren waited until Dad had set down the tray of breakfast treats and joined Mom on the couch. Dad wrapped his arm around her and kissed her cheek as she rested her head on his shoulder.

"Mom and Dad, this is for you," Darren said as he handed them the present.

It wasn't much—not very big, and definitely not very expensive—but Mom looked delighted to see Darren's gift all the same.

"Oh, honey, this is so nice," she said, running a finger along the cheery red wrapping paper. "I can't wait to see what's inside!"

Darren held his breath as he waited for his parents to open the present. He'd made the ornament himself, gluing together twigs from the old oak tree in their front yard to form a picture frame. On each corner, Darren had attached an acorn cap. One was labeled "Mom," one said "Dad," and then the two on the bottom said "Ray" and "Darren," of course. Inside the frame was this great picture of the four of them, the one Uncle Howard had taken at homecoming during Ray's sophomore year of high school. Darren had even added a loop of twine so that it could be hung on the Christmas tree.

At first, Mom and Dad didn't say anything; they just exchanged a long, loving look.

"Well, now, that is something special," Dad finally said.

"Darren, come here and give me a hug," Mom said, holding out her arms. "This is beautiful! I love it!"

"Thanks," Darren said. "I made it myself."

"You *did*?" Mom asked. "Oh, honey, it's perfect!"

Dad took the ornament and walked straight over to the Christmas tree. He did a little careful rearranging of the other ornaments, all of which were family heirlooms, until there was room to hang the one Darren had made, front and center.

"Perfect," Dad declared, echoing Mom.

Darren's grin grew even wider. There was so much love in that room—love and joy and togetherness . . .

Then it was all shattered by a sudden crash.

Darren spun around wildly, just in time to see a jaguar leap through the picture window, sending millions of shards of glass flying through the air.

Everyone screamed and started to run—Mom and Dad and Ray and Darren—all in different directions, all apart—

How will we find one another again? Darren worried.

The living room was melting away into mist. . . . Darren kept running. . . . The jaguar was chasing him now, teeth bared, claws flashing.

There was something he was forgetting, Darren was sure of it. *Think,* he told himself. *Remember.*

But he just couldn't.

Not that it mattered now. It was a perfect day for the beach—not a cloud in the sky, and a blazing sun that took the chill off the normally cold ocean water. Darren leaned back in his beach chair, closed his eyes, and wiggled his toes in the sand. Maybe in a minute he'd grab his boogie board and hit the waves, see what Ray was up to—

Splash!

As a bucket of cold salt water hit Darren squarely in the face, he realized *exactly* what Ray was up to.

"Got you! Got you! Now, what are you going to do about it?" Ray asked, doing a victory dance on the hot sand.

"You're about to find out!" Darren shot back, grinning at Ray.

"Honey! You need more sunblock!" Mom called out to Darren. "Real quick, before you get in the water."

Dad waved a shovel in the air. "I could really use some help with this sand castle," he announced. "Those turrets aren't going to build themselves."

Thud. Thud. Thud. Thud.

In rapid succession the jaguar's paws hit the sand, smashing the sand castle into nothingness as it ran across the beach.

Everyone screamed. . . .

Vanished . . .

Remember! Darren urged himself.

But he couldn't.

And then he was back in the living room, the gray and gloomy living room. Sitting next to Ray by the picture window—miraculously unbroken once more—while Mom and Dad sat as far apart as humanly possible. A heaviness settled over the four of them: the dread of what was coming, the impossibility of avoiding it.

This time no one else seemed to notice when the jaguar entered the room. *Besides, what does it matter?* Darren wondered. *Everything's already ruined.* Somehow, he already knew what was going to happen . . . as if he'd already lived through it once.

"This isn't a conversation we ever wanted to have with you," Mom began. "It's— I—"

As her voice faltered, Dad sighed. "What your mother is trying to say," he began, "is . . ."

"We've decided to get a divorce," Mom finished.

The jaguar padded across the room and sat next to Darren, almost protectively. Their eyes locked, and as he stared into the creature's gleaming golden eyes, he suddenly remembered everything.

"It's you," Darren whispered to her.

Of course it is, Gabriella thought back. *You didn't think we'd abandon you, did you?*

"I don't know what to think anymore," Darren said, and he buried his head in his hands.

Gabriella nodded toward his parents, who were sitting on the couch, motionless and oblivious. *This is it, isn't it?* she asked. *This is why your powers have been out of control.*

Darren nodded. "Yes," he said, and the word reverberated through his dream. *Yes. Yes. Yes. Yes. Yes.* An echo that only got louder each time it sounded. It was out in the open now.

It was real.

I'm so sorry, Gabriella thought. *I know how much it hurts.*

"It hurts more than anything," Darren told her. "All these happy memories we made together—at the beach, on Christmas morning, even just hanging out and watching a movie; they're slipping away. Mom is always working—even when she's home, she's always working—but at least she's here. Dad's gone. He's gone. And Ray's at college, like, all the time."

You must feel so alone.

"Because I *am* alone," Darren replied. One tear—just one—slipped down his cheek. He swatted at it angrily, hoping that Gabriella hadn't noticed.

Then, he realized, she wouldn't care. So Darren decided that he didn't care either.

You are not *alone,* Gabriella's voice rang through his head with striking clarity. *You'll always have us. We're your family now, too.*

But Darren shook his head. "We might be moving,"

he said. "Mom is looking for an apartment in New Brighton."

You think you can get rid of us that easily? Gabriella asked.

"You should get rid of *me*," Darren said. "I ruin anything good. My powers are too dangerous—I hurt you, I could've hurt Fiona. Even my own parents can't bear to live in the same house with me—"

Whoa. Hold it right there, Gabriella cut him off. She extended a paw, pointed it at Darren's parents. *You think this is your fault? Absolutely not. Was it my fault when my dad walked out?*

"No," Darren said, but Gabriella wasn't done yet.

Of course not, she replied. *But I thought it was. For months I tried to figure out what I'd done wrong. If only I'd cleaned my room without being asked. Made my bed. Set the table. And then I realized that Dad didn't leave because of me. Adults make, like, tons of mistakes. All the time. And him leaving us, well, I think that was just another big mistake that he made. And it definitely wasn't my fault.*

Darren ran his hands over his head. "But where do I even go from here? Everything's all messed up. We might move; we might not have enough money; we might not ever be together again, not the way we used to be."

You might not be, Gabriella conceded. *It will be different, but that doesn't mean it can't be good again, too.*

Darren wanted to believe that Gabriella was right, but his thoughts were still clouded with doubts and fears. "I'm just . . . I'm really tired. I don't—I don't think I have anything left. It's probably better if I stay here."

Not an option, Gabriella replied shortly. *I need you to wake up, Darren. Your powers*—

"My powers?" he echoed. He stuck out his arm and shook his hand. "My powers are a joke. This wristband is the only reason I got my powers under control. But it was a lie, too. I was just being played by another one of Auden's henchmen. Do you even realize what that means? The kind of risk I put you all in?"

You didn't mean— Gabriella began.

"What I *meant* to do doesn't matter!" Darren exploded. "What matters is what I *did*, what I could still do—at any moment, to anyone! Without the wristband, my powers will go haywire again. Electrical storms, exploding lightbulbs, bolts of lightning shooting in every direction—" Darren's voice broke. He paused, took a deep breath, and tried again. "If I'm by myself in New Brighton, how will I ever learn to control my powers?"

Listen, Gabriella thought urgently. *Do you remember when we found out we were Changers? We may be weird, but we're weird together. You have to trust us. We will always have your back, and nothing can change that—not family problems, not Auden Ironbound's dirty tricks, not even moving away. Mack and Fiona and I are here for you.*

For the first time Darren looked straight at her. "You mean it?"

Of course I do, Gabriella told him. *But you have to let us be there for you. You can't keep this stuff all bottled up inside. Trust me, I tried that when my transformations were out of control, and it only made things worse. But you know what helped? Asking for help. Talking about my problems. Keeping that stuff—fear, pain, loss—inside . . . it's like poison.*

Darren's eyes widened. Hadn't Ray told him the same thing?

The jaguar placed her paw on Darren's hand. *You got*

this, she told him. *Because we got your back. Always.*

Darren smiled, and for the first time in days, it wasn't forced. He knew, of course, that there were no magic fixes, that his parents' divorce was going to hurt for a while—probably a long while. Even so, he realized he had his friends, and that gave him hope. Maybe Gabriella was right. Maybe—even though he couldn't quite believe it right now—everything really would be okay. And that was enough, Darren realized, to keep going. To keep fighting.

He took a deep breath and looked around at the house, at his parents sitting so far apart on the couch. *It's time to leave this behind,* he thought.

And then he opened his eyes.

Chapter 12
JASPER

Gabriella gasped and bolted upright. "He's awake!" she shouted.

The web of electricity blazed with a brightness so intense that Gabriella had to cover her face. Then, all at once, it vanished. Even the massive lightning bolt that Darren had been sending into the sky evaporated. There was a tremendous crash as thousands of books hit the floor. The witches and warlocks in the room woke up, scrambling to form a defense.

Gabriella got to her feet. "Where is—" she started to say, her voice uncertain. Then she saw it: a pair of eyes, glowing red from across the room. Gabriella remembered where she had seen eyes like that before: in her kitchen, when three warlocks had shown up in pursuit of Circe's Compass. Tía Rosa had incapacitated two of them, but the third managed to cast a powerful spell. When he did, his eyes had glowed red—just the like the pair across the library.

Then, to her horror, Gabriella saw another pair of glowing red eyes.

And another.

And another.

A faint light spilled across the room as curses zinged through the air, ricocheting off the shelves. Gabriella reached out and grabbed Fiona's and Mack's hands and then dragged them down to the floor. "Stay low," she said urgently.

"What's going on?" Fiona asked.

"It's the Horn of Power," Gabriella explained. "That's why the warlocks kidnapped Darren and Jai and the others. They were harnessing their powers to repair it."

"No!" Fiona said. "Where . . . ?"

"It's there," Gabriella said, lifting her head just high enough to see the horn in the middle of the room, still on the floor beside the cracked pedestal. She could see, too, the First Four in action—Mr. Kimura, in *kitsune* form, was creating individual prisons of flames around each warlock. As a werewolf, Ms. Therian was on the attack, and Sefu had transformed into a hyena and was using his incredible strength to smash anything in his path. Yara, though still a human, had her head thrown back, and she was . . . *singing* the most exquisite melody that Gabriella had ever heard, and all the warlocks near her had fallen to the floor, writhing in pain.

"We'd better follow their lead," Mack said, gesturing to the First Four. "Let's transform and get the horn."

"But—" Fiona began.

"Don't worry, Fiona, we'll protect you," Mack interrupted her.

"Thanks," she said. "What I was going to say, though, is what about Darren?"

Gabriella glanced up again. How had she missed it before? On one side of the pedestal, Darren stood locked in battle with a tall, thin warlock. Looking back later, Gabriella wouldn't understand why just the sight of the man filled her with terror. He wasn't much to look at, dressed all in black, but there was something about his long fingers, pressed together, that gave her chills.

Or maybe it was just the malicious glee shining in his terrible red eyes . . .

And Darren . . .

Poor Darren . . .

He was trying *so* hard; even from a distance Gabriella could see that he was shaking from head to toe, channeling every last ounce of energy into his fingertips, where faint sparks crackled. It was obvious to Gabriella that he was trying to summon one more bolt of lightning, to stop the strange thin man in his tracks.

He doesn't have it in him, Gabriella thought suddenly, remembering how tired Darren had been, even in his dream. *He's been fighting these warlocks for so long, using all his energy, all his power. . . .*

Worst of all, the thin man seemed to know that too. He wasn't doing anything to even try to stop Darren. He just stood there, smiling his mocking smile, as if he enjoyed Darren's struggle.

As if it was the funniest thing he'd ever seen.

That was all it took for Gabriella's fear to be replaced

by a flame of rage. That's my *friend*, she thought angrily as she transformed into a jaguar. Mack was already in his *kitsune* form, and together, they shielded Fiona as they tried to cross the room, dodging curses and spells and terrible incantations.

Stay strong, Darren, Gabriella thought to him. *We're coming!*

Stop . . . Jasper . . . was all he could manage, and it was enough. Besides, Gabriella wanted him to save whatever strength he had left.

She had a feeling he was going to need it.

The sparks at Darren's fingers were growing fainter, fainter, fainter . . . and at the same time, his legs seemed to quiver unsteadily, as if he were about to fall.

Hurry! Gabriella thought to Fiona and Mack as they pressed forward.

They made it just in time.

Because Darren did fall; he collapsed, actually, but Fiona was ready for him. Somehow, she caught him and pulled him to safety. At least, that's what Gabriella hoped Fiona had been able to do. She couldn't think about it. Not now, not when she and Mack were all that stood between the thin man—Jasper—and the Horn of Power.

My, my.

It took Gabriella a moment to realize that Jasper's voice had slipped into her own thoughts.

Wasn't that a sight to behold? Jasper thought to her, his words sticky with sarcasm. *Very noble. Very touching.*

Mack used his powers to conjure up a small fireball, which he lobbed at the man. Jasper didn't even flinch as he dodged the blast, which fell to the ground in a smoldering heap of ashes behind him.

Gabriella's eyes never left Jasper's pinched, unpleasant face as she leaped at him, claws gleaming in the moonlight. She managed a small swipe that left him clutching his side.

Gabriella grinned and readied herself for another attack, but suddenly, she was gripped by an intense pain. A wound the same as the one she'd given Jasper appeared on her own side.

Mack! she thought to her friend. *He's using some kind of spell—any hit will bounce right back at you. We need the First Four to break it. There's no way we can take him on our own.*

Jasper seemed to realize that the kids had discovered

the spell. With a smile he walked past them to the pedestal, where the Horn of Power, now gleaming and fully repaired, lay.

Around them, the battle was dying down as Ms. Therian, Sefu, Mr. Kimura, and Yara bested the warlocks and witches, one by one. *That's the last of them*, Gabriella thought to Mack.

But even as the First Four approached, Jasper only grinned. His eyes gleamed, then glowed, as red as blood.

No! Gabriella thought. She lunged forward, but it was too late.

At that very moment, Jasper and the Horn of Power disappeared in a plume of toxic, choking smoke that spiraled into the sky.

Chapter 13
TOGETHER

Darren's face twitched; his eyes opened, and he blinked. He wasn't quite sure where he was, but familiar faces slowly came into focus: Mom on his left side, Dad on his right, and Ray perched at the end of the bed.

Another dream, Darren thought, grimacing. That was the only explanation as to why his whole family would be together like this. His meandering dreams before had led him through some of his most powerful memories: Christmas traditions, the annual family beach trip, and then the terrible talk with Mom and Dad about their divorce. And now . . . they were all in . . . a hospital? Darren had never been in the hospital before, so that didn't make sense. But then again, dreams usually didn't. Darren tried to figure it out, but his mind felt so drained. No, wait. All of him felt drained. His arms, his legs, even his head felt like they weighed a thousand pounds.

Darren glanced around warily, waiting for Gabriella to burst into the room in her *nahual* form. Then he tried to sit up. Mom and Dad reached for him at the same time—Mom's hand on his forearm; Dad's hand on his shoulder. That's when Darren realized he wasn't dreaming, after all. Nothing could be more real than their touch.

"Easy, champ," Dad said in a quiet voice. "You need your rest."

Darren sank back down onto the pillow. Just then, he heard a mechanical noise as the upper part of the bed began to rise up.

Ray, grinning mischievously, held up a small remote control. "You've hit the big-time, D," he joked. "This place has it all! Your own TV, a remote-controlled bed, and even room service. Though I can't say I would recommend the food."

Darren cracked a smile. "Very funny," he replied. "But seriously . . . why am I here? What happened?"

Mom and Dad exchanged a glance. "You collapsed during football practice, sweetie," Mom explained. "Don't worry, though; the doctors say you're going to be just fine. It's just a mild case of dehydration and exhaustion."

"Enough to give us quite a scare, though," Dad added.

Football practice? Darren thought. He tried to think back— Yes, he remembered practice now, and the urgent phone call from Fiona. Then there was . . . nothing. A gaping hole in his memory.

Suddenly, it all came rushing back: The library. The chairs. The wristband. Jai. Jasper.

The Horn of Power.

Did the warlock fix it? Darren wondered urgently. He tried to sit up again, but his father's grip was too strong.

"Please, Darren," Dad said with an unusual note of pleading in his voice. "You've *got* to rest."

But Darren barely heard him. *Where are they?* he wondered wildly, glancing around again for Fiona, for

Mack, for Gabriella, for the First Four—for *anyone* who could tell him what had *really* happened.

Then Darren forced himself to take a deep breath. *Jasper and his crew wouldn't exactly drop me off at New Brighton Memorial Hospital,* he reminded himself. *If I'm here, that means I'm safe. So, the other Changers must be safe too.* He would just have to be patient until they could tell him everything.

"We heard you were crushing it on the field," Ray was saying. "I know I told you exercise can help with stress, but seriously, D, you can't get so carried away."

"You've been through so much this week," Mom said gently. "Are you ready to talk now?"

You have no idea, Darren thought. But that heavy sense of dread that had overwhelmed him for days seemed somehow lighter. And when he tried to keep his mouth shut, the strangest thing happened: the words came all on their own.

"Everything is awful," he began. "I don't even know how to describe how I'm feeling. All the time, I feel so—so—so sad and angry and—and *betrayed.* It feels like everything is ruined. And I hate feeling like this. I *hate* it."

"That's our fault," Dad spoke up. "Your mother and I take full responsibility. We should've done a better job talking to you and Ray about the problems we were having. It was wrong to keep it from you and then just spring the divorce on you like that."

"It's hard, sometimes, to remember just how grown up you two are," Mom chimed in. "I still think it's our job to protect you boys, but this time, our attempts to protect you just made things worse." Then she sighed and squeezed Darren's hand. But he wasn't done yet.

"We used to be so happy," Darren continued. "And now it's just . . . gone. Over. What if we're never happy like that again? Everything's changing, and there's nothing I can do to stop it."

"One thing isn't changing," Dad said firmly. He looked directly into Darren's eyes. "The love your mother and I have for you boys can *never* change. *Ever*."

"And we will always be a family," Mom said, "even though Dad and I won't be married or live together anymore. You and Ray will always come first for us. We're going through a hard time right now—all of us—but we're tough. We'll survive this and be even stronger than we were before."

"This isn't the end of our happiness," Dad said. "I promise you, Darren, that we are going to make more happy memories—sometimes apart, and sometimes, even together."

"Holidays, birthdays, graduations," Mom said, ticking each one off on her fingers. "Dad and I don't want to miss anything. It's true that our family is going to look different from the way it was. And that will take some getting used to—for all of us."

Darren and Ray exchanged a glance.

"Time heals," Mom continued. "It really does. There will come a day when you suddenly realize things don't seem quite so awful. Your father and I will always be here for you, no matter what. And nothing can change that."

Her words gave Darren the courage to say what he'd been thinking.

"What about moving to New Brighton?" he asked. "I saw your laptop—"

"You saw my laptop?" Mom interrupted.

"I didn't mean to snoop," Darren said quickly. "It was right there—the website for the divorce attorney and the website with apartment listings."

To Darren's surprise, though, Mom didn't seem mad at all.

"No wonder you've been so upset," she said, squeezing his hand. "Darren, we are *not* going anywhere."

Darren blinked in confusion. "Then how come—"

"The apartment's for me, Sherlock," Ray spoke up. "I'm going to move into my own place off campus when the semester is over. No more noisy dormitory! And no more all-night study sessions in the library's quiet room."

Darren was so relieved to hear the news that he couldn't help it: he burst out laughing. So did Ray, and then Dad, and even Mom joined in. And in that moment, Darren suddenly realized the truth in what his parents had said. They would still have happy times together, even though things were forever changed.

A loud knock made everyone look over at the doorway, where Ms. Therian was standing with Mack, Fiona, and Gabriella. Darren grinned when he saw

Mack holding a bunch of get-well balloons.

"I hope we're not intruding," Ms. Therian said.

"No, not at all. We'll head down to the cafeteria to get some supper," Mom said. "But don't exert yourself too much, Darren. Remember, you need your rest."

"Fries and a chocolate shake?" Ray asked, pointing at Darren.

Darren grinned at his brother. "You know it. Thanks, Ray."

After Darren's family left, Ms. Therian closed the door behind them.

"They don't know a thing," Darren said right away. "They're not even aware I was gone."

"Yes," Ms. Therian said, nodding. "Yara used a . . . Well, let's just say she had a little . . . chat with them and all parties involved."

"A chat involving a memory-obliteration spell, I bet," Mack joked under his breath.

"Thank you," Darren said, relieved. Then he looked at Gabriella. "Did you tell everybody?"

"About your parents?" Gabriella asked. She shook her head. "No. Not my news to tell."

"What's going on?" Fiona asked.

Darren took a deep breath. "My parents," he began. "They're—they're getting divorced."

So that's what it feels like to say it out loud, Darren thought. Strangely, it wasn't as awful as he expected it would be—maybe because Fiona and Mack and Gabriella were by his side in an instant, all talking at once. He didn't have to hear their exact words to know that they were full of support.

"Guys, guys, hold on," he said. "I owe you an apology. I should've said something. But I—I didn't know how. And I was so upset that my powers went haywire—really, really haywire—and I *still* didn't say anything."

Darren paused to take a deep breath. "I didn't realize it, but I put us all in danger. And I'm sorry—more sorry than I can say. It will never happen again. I promise."

"What about . . . the move?" Gabriella asked quietly. The others stared at Darren, concerned.

"Actually, it was just a misunderstanding. We're not moving to New Brighton!"

Gabriella cheered so loudly that Darren had to shush her before a nurse could come in.

"Can you fill me in on what happened?" he asked. "I don't remember much."

"Your parents were right about needing your rest," Ms. Therian began. "You exhausted your powers in your resistance, Darren. Without your fight . . . Well, let's just say we wouldn't have been able to accomplish as much as we did when we went up against Jasper."

Darren sighed with relief. "So you got the horn," he said happily.

Ms. Therian's smile disappeared. "I'm afraid not," she said bluntly. "Though we won the battle, Jasper managed to escape with the Horn of Power."

"No," Darren began. But before he could continue, Ms. Therian held up a hand to stop him.

"All is not lost," she said. "We were able to rescue Jai and the other kidnapped younglings. They're home with their families now, safe and sound. We also took quite a few of Auden's people as prisoners. Still, we have no doubt that the Horn of Power is back in Auden Ironbound's hands. His retribution will be swift, so heal fast. It is only a matter of time before he uses the horn again."

Gabriella shrugged. "Let him try. It didn't affect us before, and it won't affect us now."

"Yes," Ms. Therian said drily. "I expect he's figured that out as well. That's why Akira believes he will come for you—all of you—first. He won't be taking any chances this time."

Darren looked her straight in the eyes and said, "And neither will we."

EPILOGUE

Fiona's phone buzzed on her bedside table. She knew it was a bit too early to be her alarm—the light spilling through her windows was still a little reddish orange, as though the sun had just barely come up.

> Hey all! Out of the hospital this morning and headed home. Feeling a lot better. See you Monday.

Fiona smiled. It was good to hear that Darren was feeling better, both inside and out. She exited out of her texts to check the time. It may have been a weekend, but that didn't stop Fiona from getting up early.

She loved to tackle her homework first thing on Saturdays; it felt good to get it out of the way and have the rest of the weekend stretch out ahead of her, wide open for anything she wanted to do. Of course, these days there was just one thing she wanted: to spend time at Broad Rock, scanning the ocean for signs of *selkies*. The battle at Elmbridge had only reinforced Fiona's conviction that she *had* to find a *selkie*, any *selkie*, to help her. Without a *selkie* to teach her their secret songs, Fiona would never truly be able to use her powers.

And that would be unthinkable.

Enough daydreaming, Fiona thought as she rolled over in bed. She reached down to the floor for her backpack.

But it wasn't there.

Fiona sat up.

That's weird, she thought, a small frown flickering across her face. She always put her backpack right next to her bed at night; sometimes, she would even lie in bed with her arm dangling over the side, just so she could feel her *selkie* cloak beneath her fingers as she drifted off to sleep. Fiona was certain that she'd put her backpack in the usual place last night.

Well . . . almost certain.

Maybe I left it downstairs, she thought as she scrambled out of bed. It would be weird, but it was possible.

And possible was all Fiona needed to push her forward. She searched the living room, the kitchen, the entryway, and even the coat closet.

But her backpack was nowhere to be found.

No, Fiona thought, panic rising in her throat. If she'd somehow lost it, with her *selkie* cloak inside, if her *selkie* cloak had again been stolen from her . . .

The thought of being trapped in her human form for the rest of her life was enough to fill her eyes with tears. To never again transform into a seal; to never again dive through the ocean, hearing that strange, sweet song that carried through the water as though sung for her and her alone . . .

Still in her pajamas, still barefoot, Fiona ran outside to her dad's car. It was a long shot; it was a desperate hope—after all, she'd taken the bus home from school yesterday—but the mere chance that her backpack was in her dad's car meant it was worth checking. She rubbed the condensation off the car windows and eagerly pressed her face against the cold, damp glass.

It wasn't there, though. In her heart, she already knew that it wouldn't be.

Why did I even think it would be in Dad's car? she asked herself angrily.

Then Fiona stopped.

Unless her *selkie* cloak hadn't been stolen by a stranger, but taken . . . by someone she loved. . . .

She hurried back into the house.

As quickly and quietly as she could—after all, Dad still might be asleep—Fiona rushed to his bedroom. The door was open a crack; enough for her to push it open a few inches more and peek inside.

That's when Fiona realized her first mistake. Dad wasn't asleep at all. And from the look of things, he hadn't slept all night.

Dad's usually immaculate bedroom looked as though a tornado had swept through it. There were old photos everywhere—on the bureau and the bed and the dresser and even the floor. Hundreds of them. Fiona didn't need to look closely to know that all the photos were of her mother.

And there, in Dad's lap, was Fiona's *selkie* cloak. He held it warily, with trepidation, like he didn't know what to do with it. Or couldn't quite trust it.

The morning sunlight touched the lovely cloak and made it gleam. Fiona longed for it. She needed it like she needed air. All her instincts told her to grab it and run, but she clenched her fists and forced herself to stay calm. That's when she thought of a new plan: *lie.*

The word ricocheted through Fiona's mind. *What choice do I have?* she wondered sickly. Then she swallowed hard and said, "Dad, I can explain what that is—"

Her voice broke off unexpectedly when her father looked up at last—a long, terrible moment when they did nothing more than stare at each other. The expression in his eyes made Fiona shrink inside herself; a heartbreaking combination of anguish, betrayal, and most of all—fear.

"I know exactly what this is," he replied.

What challenge will the Changers face next?

Here is a sneak peek at

THE HIDDEN WORLD OF
Changers

The Selkie Song!

The *selkie* cloak shimmered in the early morning sun as it spilled across her father's lap.

Give it to me, Fiona Murphy thought, her eyes fixed on the cloak. *What if . . .*

Dad tries to take it away?

Or hide it?

Or even—destroy it?

How could Fiona live without her *selkie* cloak, the most important, most precious item she had ever possessed? It didn't look like much, velvety-soft gray material with the faintest hint of a sheen, but to Fiona, that cloak was *everything*. It was the only way she could transform into her other form—a *selkie*, or seal. As a *selkie*, Fiona had been born with her cloak, but for most of her life, she'd been without it, ever since someone had taken it from her as a baby. But once she had discovered her true nature and found her cloak, buried in a battered old chest in the sand, Fiona had sworn she would never be apart from it again.

Ever.

"Dad, I can explain what that is—" Fiona began.

Her voice broke off unexpectedly when her father looked up at last, a long, terrible moment when they did nothing more than stare at each other. The expression in his eyes made Fiona shrink inside herself: a heart-breaking combination of anguish, betrayal, and most of all—fear.

"I know exactly what this is," he replied.

As the words slipped from his lips, Fiona saw her father clutch her precious *selkie* cloak even tighter. He might as well have reached into her chest and taken hold of her heart; it seemed to skip a beat.

"Please," Fiona said, her hands reaching for the cloak.

But her dad didn't give it up. He couldn't even look at her. "I have to ask," he began. "That time you were in the water—during the first week of school—"

Fiona's heart sank. *Here it comes*, she thought.

"Did you really fall in?"

A long silence followed. *Please*, Fiona thought. *Don't make me say it.*

"Or did you transform?"

"It was the first time," Fiona whispered, staring at the ground.

Dad's heavy sigh made her look up just in time to see him cover his eyes with his hand. Here she'd thought he would be mad at her—after all, Dad had just caught her in a bold-faced lie—but instead, Dad looked . . . well, *defeated.*

Fiona wasn't sure what to say next. The truth was, she'd lied because she *had* to—she'd made vows of secrecy about the very existence of Changers, people who had the ability to shape-shift into mythological animals. Fiona wasn't the only one; in fact, there were three other kids just at Willow Cove Middle School who were Changers: Darren Smith, who could transform into a massive bird called an *impundulu*; Gabriella Rivera, a *nahual* who could change into a ferocious jaguar; and Mack Kimura, a fox Changer known as a *kitsune*. Mack's grandfather was one of the First Four, a council of elders who ruled over all the Changers in the world.

Over the last few months, the Changers had been threatened by an evil warlock known as Auden Ironbound, who was determined to seize power from the First Four and control the Changers. Fiona and her friends had already engaged in several battles with Auden and his followers, but the skirmishes were much more challenging for Fiona, who hadn't learned *selkie* magic yet. The other Changers didn't need a cloak or any sort of magical object to transform, either, which was just one reason why Fiona's *selkie* cloak was so vital— why she couldn't risk losing it. . . .

"Fiona, I'm going to ask you something else, and it's essential that you answer me honestly," Dad finally said. "Have you been contacted by another Changer? Perhaps another *selkie*? Or—or—"

Or what? Fiona wondered as Dad's voice faltered.

"Or your mother?"

Fiona blinked in surprise, unsure if she'd heard him correctly. Mom had died when Fiona was three. But the very thought that there was a way, somehow, for Fiona to contact her again filled her with hope. *Can selkies communicate with the dead?* she wondered as her imagination ran wild. *Maybe that's one of their secret powers that can only be learned from another* selkie! *Maybe—*

Then Fiona's rational, whip-smart self caught up with her imagination. She had researched *selkies* constantly since she'd found out the truth about herself, and nowhere—*nowhere*—had there been even the slightest hint that *selkies* had such a power.

And since when did Dad, of all people, seem to know so much about *selkies*?

Fiona chose her next words very carefully.

"Dad," she said slowly, "why did you ask if I'd seen Mom?"

This time, it was Dad's turn to be silent.

"Dad?" Fiona asked again.

He sighed before answering at last. "Because your mother is alive—and a *selkie*, like you."

Did you LOVE reading this book?

Visit the Whyville...

IN THE MIDDLE BOOK HIVE

Where you can:

- Discover great books!
- Meet new friends!
- Read exclusive sneak peeks and more!

Log on to visit now!
bookhive.whyville.net